A Lifelong Walk
to the
Same Exact Spot

By Rob Durham

For Beth,
Thank God, you found me

Other books by author:

Don't Wear Shorts on Stage: The Stand-up Guide to Comedy

Don't Do Shots with Strangers:
The All-Inclusive Guide to All-Inclusive Vacations

Around the Block

Somebody Else's Sky

Looking towards the future, we were begging for the past.
Well, we knew we had the good things,
but those never seemed to last.
Oh, please just last.

—Isaac Brock, Modest Mouse

Contents

Short Stories   1

Part 1   2

Arm Candy   3

Sleeping Beauty   10

Strings Detached   15

Something Old, Something New   19

Part 2   21

Picking Up the Tab   23

Jump Shots   33

Windshield   35

Apartment 3C   40

Part 3   42

Withdrawal   44

Devil's Rare   48

Not Yet   51

How I Got on SportsCenter   55

Part 4   62

Best Friend   64

Dog Named Blue   73

Brain Cooks Heart   78

The Seven Gates of Hell   81

Part 5   85

Once a Year   89

Top Shelf   102

The Turn   105

The One with Sex in It   107

Part 6   113

Extra Butter   115

Whatever Works   118

A Ride Home   122

Positive/Negative   124

Part 7   132

The More You Suffer   134

More Than They'd Seen   152

Poetry   174

Before Sex   176

Why Teachers Laugh at Their Own Jokes   178

Often Me   180

Creative Nonfiction   182

Crutch   184

Why I'm a Bears Fan   187

Forgive the Teenager   192

Author's Note

I learned a wonderful concept called "composting" from Natalie Goldberg's book, *Writing Down the Bones*. The gist of her essay on composting is that much of the pain in our lives—our garbage—needs time to rest and decompose before it becomes fertile for writing. Once enough time has passed and much of the pain has subsided or disappeared, we are better suited to write about our experiences. We turn our life's garbage into compost.

This essay struck me with a profound truth. Two decades passed before I churned out my novel, *Around the Block*, which was based on some issues I dealt with in high school. My latest novel, *Somebody Else's Sky*, captures conflicts from my 20s. These books are far from memoirs, but I experienced catharsis in writing themes and lessons I wish I had grasped when I was the age of those stories' protagonists.

This book's stories cover anything I didn't scoop up in my previous works. The "what-ifs" and the "I wonders" that my writer's mind often drifts into have been composted into 26 short stories. Some of the stories I can trace to anecdotes of my youth while others are completely manufactured from theme. I hope you comprehend their message while being entertained.

You'll notice some common elements: infatuation, breakups, and even obsession. I find the moments right before and just after a relationship are the ripest for storytelling. After all, what fun is hearing about a happy couple?

I included some poetry after the stories. Of the hundred or so poems I've written, I figured a few deserved to make it to a published book. One of them I share during my stand-up comedy performances.

The creative nonfiction pieces that conclude the book are much more autobiographical. The loss of my mother, which I continue to cope with every day, is brought up in all three though I feel the essays each hold a universal message.

I've also sprinkled in some commentary. The title of the book and all of the quotes at the beginning of each section are Modest Mouse lyrics from the great Isaac Brock. He gave me verbal permission to use them, and I even had the pleasure of showing him one of his quotes in a previous book's epigram. The band's music always seemed to carry me through those former days of heartbreak.

As always, I thank you from the bottom of my heart for reading.

Short Stories

Part 1

"You're an angel
with an amber halo
Black hair and the
devil's pitchfork"

Interstate 8
by Modest Mouse

The first story, "Arm Candy," stars a comedian, so assume there's an anecdote about its origin from years ago. As a lead-off, it captures the vibe of this collection and sets the bar for the first of many twists.

"Sleeping Beauty" will send you back to those live-and-learn college years while "Strings Detached" takes on the relationship quarter-life crisis.

"Something Old, Something New" is a short, playful flash fiction set on a wedding day. Read it carefully to catch everything.

ARM CANDY

Amber wasn't the type of ex-girlfriend to fade quietly into the background. Five days after our breakup, she left a voicemail asking for the name of the bar from our second date. She changed her profile picture a dozen times that first month, each one a photo I had taken.

When I learned from a mutual friend that Amber was planning to attend one of my stand-up comedy shows, I decided to retaliate.

Enter Vanessa. This bombshell worked two cubicles over from me 40 hours a week, and I was close enough to catch a whiff of her fruity lotions every time she applied them.

My scheme didn't require much persuasion. "Want to help me with something?"

"Business or personal, Tim?" She wheeled her chair back and faced me, legs crossed.

"My ex won't leave me alone."

Vanessa brushed her dark hair over her shoulder and

smiled. She was one of those women who claimed men were afraid to ask them out, but probably turned down a handful of suitors a week. It took months to break the habit of staring at her. At Thursday's happy hour, we "fine gentlemen" always jockeyed for the seat next to her, but we dared not attempt anything because of her assertive demeanor. So yeah, this plan was a bit ballsy.

"What can I do to help?" she asked, a common phrase around the office, implying this would be business after all.

"Amber's showing up to show up to my comedy gig on Saturday, and she won't be alone. You know what I mean?" I realized I sounded like the loser in my breakup. Vanessa would think even less of me. The entire office would know about this stunt, and the guys would never let me live it down. It could even get back to Amber somehow.

"I'm listening." She wanted to hear me say it.

"I need an escort, no wait, a date, I mean—"

"You need arm candy." She placed her hands together under her chin, mimicking a praying mantis. How fitting.

"Forget it." I shook my head. "Yeah, now that I say it out loud, it sounds kind of petty."

"If you change your mind, let me know." Vanessa bit her bottom lip and slid back into her cubicle to resume her phone calls.

I considered that maybe she actually wanted in on this scheme. My unrealistic male ego was screaming at me for withdrawing my attempt. For the rest of the morning, her voice was all I could hear. Our call center was a seasonal business helping people with tax refunds, and as March and our busiest season neared, the calls increased. Even as I spoke to random callers and gave them the spiel about their refund arriving in one to two Fridays, I couldn't shake the fantasy of Amber seeing me with Vanessa. With one look, the outcome of any argument I ever lost with Amber would be overturned. Being with Vanessa would scream, "You let this one get away?"

And then there were my fears. Had Amber found some stud much better looking than me? Did he have broader shoulders and tower over six feet tall? Would his clothes all come from those fancy stores at the mall I never bothered to enter?

I didn't want Amber back, but I couldn't let her win. I glanced back over at Vanessa. She was the only woman in the office who wore heels every day. *And* an ankle bracelet. What the hell would my ex think about a woman who wore an ankle bracelet, right?

I worked like a rock star that afternoon. As I dealt with the rude phone calls, a premise for a new comedy bit came to me. A few minutes before quitting time, my phone buzzed. It was Amber.

"Are you on the show at Chuck's Pub this Saturday?"

I handled another call before texting back, "Yes."

"Cool, we're looking forward to it."

We're. The intentional plural pronoun stung.

I put my phone back in my pocket and slid my chair back into the aisle. "Hey, Vanessa?"

She turned and put a finger up as she finished a call. Then she pulled her headset off and pushed her hair behind her ears. "What's up, Hun?" One of her heels slid halfway off her foot.

My heart fluttered. "You still down for Project: Arm Candy on Saturday?"

She blew me a kiss.

***

The Saturday night showcase at Chuck's Pub regularly drew crowds of over a hundred during the colder months.

On a normal night, I wouldn't have been nervous. The larger the crowd, the easier my job became.

I hadn't dared offer Vanessa a ride to our pseudo date. Plus, I had to be at the venue early, and I didn't want her waiting alone at the bar.

When the showroom doors opened for seating, I cowered backstage with the other comics, peeking out every so often. Where was Amber going to sit? And where was Vanessa?

My stomach twisted. What if Amber didn't show and Vanessa thought I'd only asked her out as a ploy for a first date? Or worse, what if Vanessa didn't show and Amber and her new beau cornered me afterward? I was about to hurry back out to the bar when I saw my ex enter the showroom.

Her date looked underwhelming at first, but as they walked toward their seats in the second row of tables, I got a better look. He had one of those faces with an orchestrated scruff, and I could safely say his hair was cut in a fancier salon than my Great Clips. His brown leather jacket looked almost liquid.

I felt underdressed. Same old jeans. Same old polo shirt faded by too many trips through the wash. Where was *my* date?

Somehow, my set went well. The crowd was enthusiastic, and I managed to stay focused despite knowing my ex-girlfriend was probably on her third drink with a guy she'd go home with. Instead of staying backstage to support my friends, I slipped out to the bar area.

A moment later, Vanessa found me. "That was great!" she said.

"I thought you missed it."

"Sorry, a little late, but I caught your whole skit." I hated that word, but at least she witnessed it.

"Want to grab a drink out here with me then?" she asked.

She took her coat off, revealing a little black dress that was delightfully not office-appropriate. I beamed with pride as she slid into the stool next to me at the bar. She waved her french-manicured hand at the bartender. "Martini, please?"

The bartender obliged but ignored me and my nearly empty Corona bottle.

As we chatted, I forgot all about the plan, Amber, and Mr. Leather Jacket. I was on a solid first date! I didn't want the show to end or the crowd to intrude, but alas, the showroom doors finally swung open.

"My turn to perform," Vanessa announced. God bless her.

Amber and her man were the last to exit the showroom. She feigned surprise with a goofy smile when she saw me, but her shock was evident when she noticed Vanessa. She paused her strut, then linked arms with the mystery man and approached us.

"Hi there," she said, her voice dripping with fake cheer. "I'm Amber, and this is Logan." She introduced Logan to me only. "Who do we have here?"

Amber's eyebrows rose. I even noticed her staring at Vanessa's Jimmy Choo heels. She couldn't help but look her up and down. No one could.

I smiled. "This is Vanessa."

When Vanessa stood, her dress hiked up to her upper thigh. She extended her hand to Amber. It was then that I noticed the brown beer bottle, a trembling Bud Light, in my ex's other hand. She was shaking so badly, she almost dropped it. Satisfaction washed over me. I almost felt guilty. Almost. The jealousy pouring from Amber's eyes confirmed that she wasn't serious about Logan. I'd love to bottle that moment for future reference. Was she going to cry?

"How you been, Trouble?" Vanessa said to Logan.

"Good, you?" He smiled back at her. They bumped their hips. What was happening? I felt my temperature rise and my stomach drop.

Vanessa looked at me. "You two probably want to catch up a bit."

I didn't! I could've gone my whole life without ever speaking to Amber again if Vanessa had just stayed by my side. Instead, she was letting Logan pull out a chair at a nearby table for two while my ex stared at me with a look as sour as the day we broke up.

"So Logan and I have been seeing each other. You could say we're getting serious," Amber said. "Guess it's good to get this over with."

"I've known Vanessa awhile," I said. Behind Amber, our two dates laughed. Only silence joined our awkward exchange.

I don't remember what we even talked about after that, then suddenly Logan was putting his jacket on.

"Heading to the ladies' room," Vanessa said, touching my shoulder.

I nodded, glad to be noticed again.

Amber trailed Logan by a few steps as they left without a goodbye.

I waited. Vanessa was taking her sweet time in the restroom. There wasn't a line. Had she gone back into the showroom?

I was ordering another round when Amber walked back in.

"Well, this sucks," she said, sitting down in Vanessa's spot.

"Um, that seat's taken," I said, not needing to rub it in

further. "She's still in the—"

"Wake up, dummy. They left together. I need a ride home."

SLEEPING BEAUTY

I shouldn't have agreed to the whole thing, but when you're drunk . . . you know how it is. I found Ted downstairs near our blaring stereo. I turned it down since half the living room was empty. Most of our crew abandoned our keg for a slice of pizza down the street or an after-hours party along frat row.

Ted was mid-conversation, but I interrupted, doing his pals a favor. I doubt any of them cared about the charity 5K he was organizing. He squashed a can and flipped it into the trash barrel we'd brought inside.

"She's passed out. Upstairs," I said.

"Who?" he asked.

He knew who. She was the main reason he threw the party to begin with. Anything to see her. His excuse that dates were "too awkward" and "too direct" actually made sense in our circles. Every couple we knew started as a drunk hookup, that turned into a habit, that turned into a relationship. Three parts alcohol, two parts college body, and that was the recipe for the person who you spent a portion of your twenties with.

"Justine. She's passed out on your mattress." Notice I didn't say bed. Ted's lair was eighty square feet of textbooks, socks (some clean, some dirty), and a futon mattress pushed against the corner so that he had room for a dresser to *not* put clothes into.

"Are you sure?" He tried to sound concerned, but his smile revealed something else.

"Sure that it's her? Or that she's passed out?"

"Sorry, dumb question."

I followed him two steps at a time. The apartment had three floors with two bedrooms and a bathroom on the second and third floors. Our second-floor roommates wisely kept their bedrooms closed during a party like this. At the top of the steps, Ted peeked into his own room as if he was a trespasser. The hall light illuminated just enough.

I stayed back a bit as Ted absorbed the situation. I understood what he saw in her. She lay on her stomach with one arm tucked under his pillow. Her jeans hugged her waist and the bare inch of skin on her side made a great focal point.

"I guess this isn't the way you planned it," I whispered.

Ted playfully backfisted my shoulder. "What am I supposed to do?"

I wasn't sure if he was purposefully loud so that she'd wake up or if he was just too drunk for volume control.

I shrugged. "I know what you *shouldn't* do." Again with his backfist.

"Justine?" He was quieter this time. He didn't want to wake her up just yet. His eyes continued to scan her. She'd kicked off her shoes which sat near a tangle of chargers. The strap of her black top had slid towards her bicep. Her brown hair scattered all over his pillow. Not that he washed his sheets much before, but now I knew they'd never see the laundromat.

Ted continued to stand there, wavering. I took a step back, opening the doorway completely. It felt like minutes before he finally walked in and knelt next to her. I disappeared further into the hallway, my regret overridden by curiosity. God, my poor chum was so in love.

I listened to him. "Justine? Are you okay?"

Only a deep breath from Ted.

"I wish I could say the things I want to say while you're awake."

That statement tore me up a little. Ted had been lovesick for almost the entire semester. He met Justine through some friends and one night as a group all walking home from a party, they held hands. It took him weeks just to find her again, but with enough social networking and then an exchange of DMs, Ted fell ass over heels for Justine who happened to be the cousin of the girl he ended parties with all of last year. Shitty odds if you ask me.

"I know you don't think it could ever work between us, but since I met you . . ."

Part of me wanted to disappear back downstairs, but I couldn't give him the privacy he deserved. I'd heard him talk about Justine so many nights, I felt like I deserved to hear how this turned out. It's not like I was learning anything new.

I dared myself and then finally peeked in. Ted knelt with a hand extended but wasn't touching her. I promise, the guy wasn't a creep. I mean, what would you do if the love of your life, or at least your junior year fall semester, was asleep on your bed? And before you decide, drink about a dozen beers and *then* make that decision.

It was almost cute the way he wouldn't let himself penetrate an invisible force field . . . on his own bed. I could tell he'd forgotten about me as he continued. "I'd make you so happy every day. I don't even know what I'd ever have to complain about or worry about. Every time there's a party and you're there, I try to play it cool, but I could just look at you all day. You're just so . . ."

I considered walking in, but he stopped talking. I heard some movement, so I counted to ten and took another peek. Ted had covered her with his blanket and curled himself up on the floor. A big baby, drunk, dumb, and in love. But considerate. I began to feel even worse. This shouldn't have happened, and it was my fault. If nothing else he was going to hurt his back again and our intramural basketball team wouldn't have our center for our semifinal game.

More time passed, but I knew he was still wide awake. When Ted dozes, he snores a little. When he sleeps after drinking, the neighborhood can hear it. I sat down with my back to the wall beneath our Budweiser poster. It was quiet for a long time until I heard one of his joints crack as he stood up.

"You're just too beautiful. I can't take it." I heard him walk across the room.

Now I was the one who felt vulnerable, still slumped in the hallway over a half-hour after I'd escorted him up. The voices downstairs had faded and someone's trip-hop playlist had taken over the speakers. I did my best acting job and closed my eyes. "Oops, I nodded off. Everything okay?"

He nodded yes with a tired, dejected look.

"Sleep in my room if you want," I said. "Unless . . ."

"I'm just gonna have a few more downstairs," Ted said. "I can sleep on the couch once everybody goes. Maybe give her a ride in the morning so she doesn't look like the walk of shame."

"That would be nice of you," I said. "You're a good dude, Teddy. Just be patient. It'll happen if it's supposed to."

He nodded and headed down the steps carefully holding the railing.

I waited for the song downstairs to end and then entered. "He's gone," I said.

Justine sat up, pushing her hair back from her face. "Oh my god."

Her makeup was smeared around her puffy eyes.

"I told you," I said. "I fucking told you."

STRINGS DETACHED

A person can become a habit, like smoking. It starts with a casual decision, a drunken "What's the harm?" moment when you crave a distraction. But then there's a follow-up a weekend or two later, again fueled by alcohol and an unburdened spirit, but with a hint of intention. Soon, it's a weeknight rendezvous after a Wednesday happy hour.

You told me upfront, "No strings attached." A throwaway phrase, easy to mumble while buttoning back up. Anything to make the other person feel better about their impulses.

And those morning conversations, when the light slips through the blinds and you turn away to mask bad breath and shame? They lay the foundation for your unspoken agreement, your state-of-the-union address delivered in a stumbling mess of sentences to appease the partner you swear it's over with, but deep down, you know it's not.

"Sorry, I'm on the rebound, you know . . ."

"Yeah, I just need some space to have fun and . . . whatever."

"Okay, yeah, so we—"

"Oh definitely. Yeah, don't think I'm like all, you know."

Mutual fake laughter.

The token conversation simultaneously means so much and nothing. A tip-toe of intimacy where at least one person has fingers crossed, promising not to make any promises.

The one who ends up hosting these sleep-with-me-overs owns the heart less likely to catch feelings. I suspected this as you and I had fallen into a routine that bordered on a relationship.

You weren't the one. I liked your body, but I wanted no part of the family you harped about or the wounded credit score you alluded to. Maybe if you were two years younger, I could've forgiven it, but I wasn't labeling my life stable either. At 27, I still didn't have a bed frame or health insurance, so knowing I was the responsible one doomed our chances. Our need for each other was simple: Tuesday evenings ("I should probably go before it gets too late"), sometimes Thursdays if you had Friday off ("Do you care if I just . . ."), and almost every Saturday (though you always arrived technically Sunday morning).

You didn't leave a toothbrush in my bathroom but carried one in your purse, understanding the stigma. Your gloves rented a space on my counter. My cat greeted you every time. You'd help yourself to the fridge. No key, no kiss goodbye, no conversations about *us*.

It started a week after the Super Bowl and carried into May.

"You have to go to a friend's wedding? Have fun. Yeah, I can give you a lift afterward if you need."

"You're right, I don't like that band. Good call, I would've been a buzzkill to your friends."

"Are you working a double? Text me if you're bored."

On we went, not meeting each other's people and ignoring the other languages of love.

Physical touch, physical touch, physical touch, physical touch, physical touch. Words of affirmation? We were just kidding.

"Aww, you brought me a sandwich you barely touched. What a gentleman."

"Yeah, I've seen it, but I'll watch it again."

They weren't favors; they were sarcastic gestures on a two-way street.

"Thanks, dork. You shouldn't have."

Maybe it was a long hair you left in my sink or a dream I had about someone else. One day, I explained that I'd had enough. You nodded along, stunned into silence.

No, I wasn't kidding. We needed to stop.

You paused again, waiting for me to smile. I didn't. I couldn't.

"Sorry," you blinked and sob-laughed. "Okay, not sure why I'm crying," you choked out. "It's not like I—"

"And that's the thing," I said. "You deserve more than this. With someone."

"I know." Again with your laugh I'd heard in every other context. "I don't know why I'm so emotional. Probably just about to start—hey, at least I'm not pregnant."

We both had a reason to laugh. The tension pretended to ease.

A bit of silence then a sniffle. The cat didn't understand and stood half-curled around the bedroom door.

You wiped your face and exited rather tersely as expected, closing the door a little louder.

Outside, a truck backed up and a car alarm wailed in the distance. My ears waited for your comment, but of course, you were gone. I looked at my phone, red battery because you needed my charger for the night.

I rolled onto my side and pressed my face against "your" pillow. Your surviving scent made me realize I definitely loved you.

SOMETHING OLD, SOMETHING NEW

With his tuxedo ready for final inspection, James tugged on his dress socks until they fit comfortably. Five years ago, he'd lost his virginity while wearing them, courtesy of Marie. They normally stayed buried in his top drawer, and neither the elasticity nor the memory had faded much. Every time he put socks away, he'd let himself relive that warm, spring afternoon he finally got lucky.

He secured his cufflinks, a pair of lucky horseshoes he'd received as a groomsman's gift when Marie's brother Ron tied the knot. They were so close back then, but after Ron's twins were born, the afternoons of watching football from his buddy's giant couch became extinct, and the friendship morphed into a sort of taboo.

They weren't necessarily lucky, but he decided long ago that his favorite boxer shorts would be worn at the altar. Marie bought them for Halloween one year. Ghosts and bats and witches and hearts. Halloween was still three weeks away, but he could justify it as seasonal if his bride asked.

The gold watch on his wrist was a good luck charm. Marie surprised him with it on his 23rd birthday. She said she felt bad because they had only begun dating and she didn't get him much when he turned 22, so she went all out. "The man I'm going to spend my life with needs to look sharp and show up on time," she said as he unwrapped presents in bed. He'd never forget the smell of the morning breeze that blew through her screen windows in that old apartment. Everything was simple back then.

"James, you ready?" the photographer called.

"I am."

They'd made the decision to take the wedding photos before the ceremony as a courtesy to the guests. The reception was expensive enough, and they figured they could save a couple of hours this way. Instead, there'd be an unveiling ceremony. The bridesmaids surrounded her with balloons of white and pink before releasing them into the air. His bride glowed in beauty as he nervously adjusted the watch on his wrist.

She spoke first. "Are you sure this is okay? You don't think it's bad luck?"

"You know I'm not superstitious, Danielle." He took a step back to gaze at the woman in the white dress before him. "There's nothing that could come between me loving you the rest of my life."

Part 2

"Your heart felt good
It was drippin' pitch and
made of wood
And your hands and
knees
Felt cold and wet on the
grass beneath"

Third Planet
by Modest Mouse

I grouped this next bunch because all four are based on real events. "Picking Up the Tab" was inspired by an acquaintance who accidentally texted me (we've all made that mistake!). "Jump Shots," though brief, is based on a summer crush from my youth. "Windshield" also stems from my younger days though its main character earns a different outcome. Apartment 3C happened during my freshman year at Ohio State while I was learning to make new friends.

PICKING UP THE TAB

Ever have the fate of someone's marriage at the tip of your fingers? I have. And it's all because I got stuck at the longest red light in the city. I was five minutes late for this dinner my pal and his wife set up, which was also a double date, which was also a blind date, which was also the fourth time they'd tried this for me. Guess they got sick of me as a third wheel. What can I say, finding a soulmate is impossible these days.

I tried to be on time, but I had to deal with the disgruntled parent of one of my third-grade students. So during this stoplight that changes about as often as the Cubs have a good season, I whipped out my phone and messaged, "Running late, sorry, accident on my route." I sent it to Nathan first, but his phone replied Do Not Disturb.

To be safe, I texted his wife Stephanie too. Surprisingly, she didn't text back right away. Miss Type A always has her phone in her hand and is the promptest person I know. I zoomed through a few more blocks of Thursday evening rush hour and finally parked at Diablo's Cantina That's when my phone buzzed back with a reply from Stephanie.

"Wish it was just me and u tonight."

Whoopsie, Steph! I was the last person she wanted to be alone with. She'd erroneously replied to my message about being late. I figured I'd bust her chops about it during dinner if the date was going south. She was probably just trying to sweet-talk Nathan into . . . something. The man gave her *everything* she wanted. She had him trained from the second or third time they met up. With looks like hers, I couldn't blame him. I had high hopes her friend would look just as hot, minus the stern attitude.

After parking, I weaved through the land of $30 burritos (you read that right) and finally located my party in the corner, seated beneath one of those neon gold Corona signs. Grease seemed to float in the air, but once I caught a glimpse of my date, I summoned my A-game.

You know those women they show in the stands whenever one of those South American soccer teams is playing in a big game? Long dark hair and a July tan? She was a Brazil jersey away from that exact look.

We had one of those mob-boss corner booths large enough to fit an entire family of Catholics, so like a child I had to slide halfway down, my ass squeaking against the vinyl before we shook hands.

"Angela," she said.

"Charmed. I'm Davis."

"Davis," she repeated. People often did this, I guess to confirm I didn't say David. I exchanged hellos with Stephanie and Nathan and then scanned the menu. Stephanie already had hers closed and was back on her phone.

"Sorry," she said. "Scheduling thing." She looked back at me. "Don't worry, we already ordered a pitcher of top-shelf marg while we waited on you."

Had I been in my typical role as a lonely, third wheel, I

24

would've asked what "thing" she had to schedule. Stephanie didn't work; she volunteered a handful of hours per week at the elementary school where I taught. She was known for killer bulletin boards, the loudest (and only) high heels in our building, and patronizing comments: "You educators are working so hard today!" or "You're making such a difference in these kids' lives."

Yeah, yeah, but when her little Stephan (yep, that's his name) got knocked down near the swing set and no one knew who the culprit was, she sang a different tune. "Someone will lose their job for this!"

Still, I had Stephanie to thank for my smoking-hot date. I started on the chips and salsa and narrowed down my order to either the grilled pork steak or the enchiladas verdes when my phone buzzed again.

"Plus we're out with his friend on a double date."

A chunk of salsa plopped onto my menu. I looked up at Stephanie. She placed her phone back into her lap, completely oblivious to what she'd done. Then she gave a sharp smile as she touched her husband's arm.

I checked the previous text to calculate the mishap. Who were these messages for?

I glanced back over at Stephanie. The way she appeared to be interested in her husband's anecdote angered me. I recognized her expression as the same one she made when she feigned interest in the kindergarten teacher. *Look how genuine my concern is. I'm a saint for giving you this much attention. If you were as hot as me you wouldn't need this job.*

Maybe I'd hated Stephanie all along for a good reason. Nathan wasn't my best friend, but he certainly deserved to know he was being cucked.

"You're awfully quiet," Angela said to me. "I guess you like the chips?"

I'd consumed half the basket and monopolized the salsa

without even thinking about it. "Sorry," I said. "Guess I'm eating away all the stress from today. Sure could use that margarita."

"Well, good news," Nathan said. The server showed up, and my wish was granted. "Rough day at work, buddy?"

I was still sucking down my first gulp when Stephanie jumped in. "Yeah, are those nine-year-olds too much for you?" She made a pouty face and looked at Angela for a laugh but didn't get one.

Had it been my third margarita, I probably would've outed her right then. "Tell me, Stephanie . . . How do you fit over two hours of volunteer work and an affair between your busy schedule of yoga and wine?"

I refrained. Instead, I gave my best stone-cold glare. The one that causes my students to quiver. It triggered her into an extended drink through her straw.

The server returned with another round of chips and salsa and then took our order. "I can barely read this menu," Stephanie said. "The print is so tiny." The rest of us waited before she finally asked for one hard taco, no tomatoes, with guac on the side.

"The kitchen is a little backed up tonight, so should I get started on a second pitcher for you guys?"

Stephanie nodded yes. "I'm going to go powder my nose. Come with, Angela."

Nathan and I both slid around the booth to let the ladies out and then sat back down.

"Well?" he asked.

"Too soon to know," I said. "Definitely the most attractive blind date, but we'll see." We returned to our seats. "How's everything going with you and Stephanie?"

"Really well, thanks. I guess we've made some breakthroughs recently."

"Oh yeah?"

26

"Just being more honest and open. Focusing a lot on what's best for Stephan helps too."

I choked down another chip. "Glad to hear. Hopefully, this Angela is a keeper, and we can have more nights like this." I wouldn't jump to conclusions and out his wife tonight, no matter how badly Stephanie pissed me off.

Our ladies returned. "Full confession, we did a shot at the bar," Stephanie said. It was as if someone turned her volume up three levels.

Angela laughed. "It wasn't our fault."

God, she was hot. I was the one on a date with her, yet some other man was trying to get her drunk. No wonder she was friends with Stephanie. This connection wasn't going to be up to me. Nothing ever was. Women decide everything and usually get their way.

The image of Stephanie cheating on Nathan wouldn't fade. My stomach twisted a bit, which helped my effort to chill on the chips and salsa. The affair was probably happening in the home Nathan worked so hard for. Was it one of my coworkers? Doubtful. She didn't respect any of us educators enough to take her clothes off for them.

Maybe I was ignoring all the factors. Perhaps it was just a girlfriend she'd rather hang with instead of her husband. As our second pitcher arrived, I convinced myself I was overthinking it. Stephanie wouldn't cheat on him, and she'd certainly be more careful if she was.

Just then, Stephanie knocked her fork off the table. "Oopsy!"

"More like tipsy," Nathan said. "Guess I'm driving you home."

"But I drove Angela," she said.

Right then would have been the perfect spot for the food to arrive, but it didn't. We all went mute, pondering the obvious. Suddenly, I was an inexperienced teenage boy.

Was I supposed to offer or was that too forward? Another moment went by, and Angela checked her phone. Then even more silence.

"I can give her a lift." I slid my glass away as if I wouldn't dare finish it.

"Don't say it like she's not here," Stephanie said. She softened her tone. "And Angela, that's up to you, Hun."

I rolled my eyes. "Angela, dear. New light of my life. If you would require a ride home due to your friend's intoxication, please allow me the honor."

She laughed so hard even the table next to us knew her answer.

"Such a smartass," Stephanie said. I placed my hand in the pocket with my phone. It was now a six-shooter waiting to be drawn.

"I would appreciate it," Angela said.

"Careful what you sign up for, Davis. She lives way over in the nicer part of town."

I was now convinced Stephanie brought her attractive friend not to help me find love, but to show me why I didn't deserve it.

A server passed by with a sizzling tray of fajitas. A blender buzzed from the bar. The silence at our table turned into a game of chicken. Stephanie lost.

"Plus it's a school night. We'll drop her off since she's closer to us. Seriously." She slurred the word "seriously" into five syllables.

Angela looked helpless. How were the two even friends? And why was Nathan married to such an obnoxious woman? Maybe the affair was a blessing.

"I don't want to be any trouble. I can get an Uber," Angela said.

Nathan spoke up. "Hey, the food's not even here yet. Why are we worried about getting home?"

I looked to Angela hoping to exchange one of those tacit glances, but she was fidgeting with her napkin. Nathan felt the tension too. "I can haul everyone home since I drove the Escalade," he said. "Anyone need another shot?"

"I'm good," I said. "I'll DD if you want to let loose." He'd need more than a few shots if I decided to bring up you-know-what.

Stephanie snorted. "Can you imagine the four of us trying to fit into his car?"

I resumed drinking. "It's a Focus."

"Exactly." She took another long suck from her straw. "Now, back to these shots you mentioned." Stephanie raised her hand. "Excuse me, señor? Amigooo! Can we get more shots por favor? Cuervo clear-o."

"Blanco," I said.

"What?"

"Blanco, not clear-o."

Less than a minute later, four shots were placed on our table. I looked to Angela. She shrugged and took one.

"I'll do his," Stephanie said. She reached over, knocking a few chips onto the table.

"You can have mine," I said, looking at Nathan, but he was looking at Stephanie.

"Who are you texting?" Nathan asked.

"Oh, one of the parents." She gulped down her shot with her free hand. "Hold on, sorry."

I held my breath. I noticed how she casually angled the phone away from her husband's view.

"Oooh," Nathan said, giving her the eyebrows. "What's his name?"

"For your information, he's one of the dads in our little parent volunteer group. His name is David."

That's when it made sense who she thought she was texting. And it was the perfect cover story. Who would tell

29

their spouse the name of their lover? I returned to silent mode as the evening (and Stephanie's rambling) carried on.

The food arrived closer to an hour after we ordered, and I lost track of how many pitchers we'd drained. I kept my wits about me as did Nathan, but the ladies were both hammered. Once the plates were cleared, they excused themselves to the restroom, and somehow the seating arrangement altered so I was near Nathan and Stephanie was next to Angela. Had I just been the third wheel, I would have bailed way earlier. The question about rides resurfaced right as the check was dropped.

I attempted to calculate the tab in my head. Three entrées over twenty bucks each, Stephanie's stupid taco, at least five pitchers of top-shelf margaritas, and four shots of tequila equated to nothing a teacher's salary should have to cover. The check sat there in the middle, untouched, but only for a moment.

"Here, Davis," Stephanie said. She lunged forward so far into the table she exposed herself as she slid the leather bill folder into my lap.

I accepted with a grimace.

"You want me to get that?" Nathan asked. Angela was watching closely.

"No, it's fine," I said. "You introduced me to such a beautiful woman, it's the least I can do."

"Damn right!" Stephanie said.

Beyond intolerable.

"Unless you wanna snag this one, Steph?"

She stuck her teeth out and squinted. "Nope. And your chica is riding back with us."

Angela shrugged.

"I'll just calculate the tip." I pulled my phone out and went to the errant text thread.

Right under her message about how she'd rather be with

him, I typed, "You sure you don't want to pick up the tab? I'd rather drive Angela home." Hitting the send button never brought me so much joy.

Stephanie didn't respond right away. She was busy licking the last of the salt off the rim of her glass. I leaned back in the booth and exhaled as I watched Stephanie check her phone.

I think it was the way her eyes doubled in size that I enjoyed most. She tried to take a drink from her empty glass and almost fumbled it into her lap.

"Maybe tonight could be my treat," she said.

"Now why would you do that?" I fanned myself with the bill folder.

"I did most of the damage on the drinks."

"Can't argue with that. In fact, I think I'm still fine to drive, so . . ." I returned the check to the middle of the table.

Stephanie slid her way over and reached across her husband, grabbing it like a prize. She pulled a credit card out of her clutch. "So, you can drive Angela home?"

"I can drive you two home if you need. Or if you want an Uber?"

"I'll be okay in a few minutes," Nathan said. "You two can go."

I fake laughed. "Maybe have that David guy come get you!"

Stephanie's glare was the chef's kiss to my night.

I pulled some cash from my wallet. "I'll cover the tip."

I had no idea what to expect when I escorted Angela to my car. What kind of man hands the check back to a woman? Like a gentleman, I opened her door first. After I buckled myself in and was about to ask for her address, she turned to me.

"She and that David guy are . . ."

I smiled and nodded.

She laughed and clicked her seatbelt. "Next time just you and me, okay?"

JUMPSHOTS

If Jason Bradley was going to live up to the legacy his older brother left behind, he'd need to develop a jump shot.

While practicing on the second day of summer, he noticed her blond hair across the park after an errant free throw kicked his ball toward the swings. Her little brother fussed at something, but Jason swore that she gave him a smile before departing.

So, the next day he returned. And the next and the next and the next.

No luck.

He found her in the yearbook, a grade lower, which of course was socially acceptable, even as a freshman, but he couldn't wait until fall. The heart of a teenager has no patience.

The sun peaked in June, burned him in July, and smothered him in August, and still, he practiced, only varying his time by fifteen minutes here or there just in case she ventured onto his territory again.

And then one day, she did. Oddly enough, he didn't

even notice until she was almost on the court with him. She was alone.

Her hair was blonder, her skin a little redder, but she'd matured in the face since that yearbook photo that served him like a wallet picture sent to a soldier in Nam.

The ball almost bounced off his foot as he tried to calm himself. He'd played in packed gyms, but never had his arms shaken like this.

"You're Jason, right?" she said.

He tested his voice box for cracks, a habit he'd developed over the summer, but found that he could only nod.

"Can I shoot one?"

"Sure," he said. His brother would be proud. A bounce pass met her at the waist. She dribbled, not well, and then took a shot using equal parts right and left hand, but with that face, she was forgiven. It almost went in too.

He rebounded. "Don't worry about it. The damn rim's crooked."

"Do *not* swear around me," she said.

He waited for her to say she was kidding. She didn't. She threw up another brick and said goodbye.

As she walked away, he took a drink. The ice in his water bottle had already melted. What a dork, that one.

He happily dismissed every feeling, his heart in remission. His once again.

But man, what a hell of a jump shot he developed.

WINDSHIELD

The tires on Mitch's Jetta skidded as he turned into the east entrance of the Highlands Mall parking lot. His wipers no longer squeaked as the snowfall had thickened. Across the lot, a gray pickup plowed the powder into piles, though the asphalt disappeared under a fresh white blanket almost instantly.

The dashboard clock read 7:56. The moon rose somewhere behind a thick blanket of clouds. Shoppers hurried to their vehicles, and the familiar Midwest winter soundtrack of scraping and revving surrounded Mitch as he parked. Krista's car sat where it normally did, five rows left of the entrance near Macy's. A two-inch layer coated her red Civic.

Mitch shifted into park, turned off the ignition, and prepped himself for the brutal cold. Was there an easier method to display chivalry? He could send her flowers anonymously at work or wait patiently, say, another three or four months until maybe she would be single again.

No, her car was buried. A hero was needed.

His zipper pinched his chin and produced a spot of blood he wiped away with a glove. Where was his sock hat? He searched the backseat but never found it. His ears would punish him for that as soon as he exited his car.

The snow blew sideways now—pellets against his face. He was doing the right thing by sparing her from this frigid torture. She wouldn't know how to properly thank him. She wouldn't be able to because of her boyfriend, Quinn, who didn't need to know about any of this. Mitch didn't loathe Quinn, but he felt (and knew) he was a better fit for Krista.

A nearby SUV drove by spewing an oily exhaust. The wind howled through the layers he'd worn as he opened his trunk to retrieve his tool for the task: a $19.99 scraper from Lowe's, the best money could buy. He drew it like a sword and began removing the clumped flakes from Krista's car.

He didn't rush, hoping to time it so that as she arrived in a few minutes, he would be finishing up. Despite the ongoing blizzard, she would melt into his arms and press her cold cheek against his. A sincere hug. The idea warmed him as he continued the meticulous brushing. A drop of blood from his chin dropped into the snow, but it wouldn't slow him down.

First, he swept the snow from the front windshield and hood. Next, the entire passenger side. The driver-side windows weren't as bad, but he gave them as much care as he did his face during his morning shave. The front and back windshields would be the challenge. A layer of ice had consumed them.

More and more vehicles exited the lot. Poor Krista. Probably stuck with one last appointment at her salon: a grouchy housewife who needed her roots darkened or a bratty kid who wouldn't sit still. Mitch's good deed would brighten her otherwise terrible workday. It wouldn't happen overnight, but thoughts of him would chip away at her current relationship like the ice he currently struggled against.

Harder and harder he scraped. "Dammit," he said as he jammed his wrist while fighting the stubborn glaze. An injury from two months ago resurfaced. He'd strained it carrying too many grocery bags at once. He shortened his jabs, and eventually the front windshield cleared up. Only fresh flakes appeared on it now. He could see inside her car. Someday he'd be her passenger.

He shifted his efforts to the back window. Another gust stung his ears, his wrist ached, and his chin dripped another spot of blood. She was worth it. He paced back and forth a bit but then stumbled on a pothole. He caught his balance before rolling his ankle, but his relief was ruined by a penetrating chill. A puddle of salty slush soaked through his shoe, drenching his sock and soaking his foot.

The anger only drove him to scrape harder. He favored his right wrist as the left became useless. The cold in his drenched foot spread a chill throughout his body. The pain on his chin throbbed with each pulse.

He was doing the right thing. It had to be ten minutes past quitting time as he completed his task. He limped a lap around her car, carefully brushing off new dustings of snow.

A job well done.

He considered leaving then. Krista would be left to wonder who performed this heavenly deed. She'd ask Quinn about his whereabouts, but the sucker wouldn't know what had happened. Mitch would keep this secret in his back pocket for the perfect time. After a few drinks at a party. Or maybe a drunk text when there was trouble in paradise. She could even figure it out herself, and the ball would be in her court.

Mitch's hypotheticals were interrupted by the arrival of an immaculately clean, black Ford Bronco. Its shine preserved from the weather by a garage, Mitch imagined.

Quinn hopped out.

Mitch walked back to his car. "I was leaving the mall, so I . . ."

Quinn circled to the back of Krista's Civic. He dragged a bare hand across the trunk.

"I see what you did," he said. "Or what you're trying to do anyway." He stood gloveless with his arms folded.

The two stared at each other, separated only by another surge of horizontal snowfall.

Krista, a bundle of scarf and coat, scurried up to Quinn. "Oh my gosh, thank you guys!"

"You're welcome," Quinn said. "I enlisted some help because Mitch was here . . . for some fucking reason."

Krista peeked at him from her hood. "What happened to your chin? Is it bleeding?"

"I'm okay," Mitch said.

"Okay, well thanks again," Quinn said. "You know though," he turned to Krista, "maybe it would be safer if I just drove you to my place. It's supposed to calm down, and I can bring you back here in the morning for work. I mean, my truck's already warm, so . . ."

Krista didn't even answer. She popped open the door and climbed into the truck leaving the two guys left to exchange one more stare.

Quinn smiled and then got into his truck. Mitch didn't move until the Bronco was out of vision.

His chin hurt. His wrist hurt. His foot was soaked with cold.

Something else hurt worse.

He returned to his car and wiped the fresh snow off his windshield. When he pulled on the handle, he realized he'd locked himself out.

APARTMENT 3C

I scanned the living room of my new friends. Carson's eyelids fluttered as he nearly dozed off on his loveseat. Both roommates retired to their bedroom, and the girls held their coats and announced they were waiting on an Uber. I offered to drive them home, but they declined. Still, I had fit in. A success! We'd gone to the cinema and grabbed burgers at a diner. It didn't matter that I'd spent fifteen bucks on a crap movie; it was a win not to sit alone in the theater for once. One of the girls even laughed from across the booth at my french fry joke.

The evening still felt young, but just to me, I guess.

"We'll get drinks and have a real night out next time," Carson told me. "Looks like everyone's pretty zonked out." He yawned, and the girls put their coats on and stared at their phones.

I said my goodbyes and floated down three flights of stairs. How many times would I scale these steps to hang out with my new crew? They'd give me a nickname, set me up with one of their friends (if neither of the girls were interested), and we'd bond over coffee by day and whiskey by night. They would be my people, and maybe my 20s would stop feeling so goddamn lonely.

A draft kicked up from the open door at the bottom of the building's stairwell. My jacket. I could just grab it next time I was over, but then again, it was chilly outside, so I climbed back up to 3C, my footsteps loud on the wooden stairs. I didn't bother to knock as it had only been a minute since my departure.

I opened the door. Carson held a bottle opener. His roommates knelt by the PlayStation. Both girls held beers, and the coats they had been wearing now rested on the couch. Right next to my jacket.

I deleted Carson's number on my way out.

Part 3

"Cheer up baby
It wasn't always quite so bad
For every venom then that came out
The antidote was had"

Spitting Venom
by Modest Mouse

The next few pieces break from my usual conventions beginning with "Withdrawal" which serves as the sequel to the earlier piece, "Strings Detached." "Devil's Rare" is a spooky story (with an easter egg from my novel *Somebody Else's Sky*) that I shared at our annual Halloween party. "Not Yet" touches on infatuation with strangers and making the first move. Whether you enjoy baseball or not, "How I Got on SportsCenter" has one of the funniest endings in the collection. It was a plot I thought about for years before finally penning into a tale.

WITHDRAWAL

It's called "quitting cold turkey" because when an addict goes through withdrawal, the skin gets goosebumps resembling refrigerated turkey. That's the closest I can describe the sensation I experienced when I saw you three weeks later. It wasn't even my heart, just the rest of me that shivered. I'd imagined this encounter so many times, awake and asleep, it must have triggered that law-of-attraction bullshit. Or maybe we both tried to find a hangout we thought the other would never be. Either way, someone should invent a new idiom for how I felt.

They say you shouldn't drink alone. There were strangers around me, so technically I wasn't. That's the logic I used when I plopped onto a barstool. I'd heard the place made an exquisite Manhattan. It sounds like an excuse, and maybe it is, but I certainly wasn't there to interlope.

What troubles me is the attraction I felt when I saw you in my peripheral—a reflex before I even recognized you. Your top was so white, like something a princess would wear, and now you were blonde. "Look at her!" my heart screamed, and then the realization that it was you who sent me into a twist of panic and fascination. What had I done, releasing you?

I conjured all the negatives about you that I could. Hogging the bed, waking me up early to leave . . . Why were these dealbreakers? I couldn't think of my reasoning, but instead, noticed you were by yourself. I gulped half of my overpriced drink and plucked the cherry from its stem to establish I'd been there long before you, my night in medias res. I came to this place by myself, and you showed up purposely or coincidentally, but maybe it was a sign that breaking the habit of each other was folly.

How much more intense would a night together be after this hiatus? I'd already conceded I wouldn't be able to turn you down. An addict strapping on the tourniquet. Or maybe we just needed one more time and then I'd go back to that unfeeling I possessed the morning I said no more.

You didn't notice me at first. You looked at your phone as people who are alone in public always do. There was an empty barstool three spots to my right, but you weren't interested in a seat. A man with a shaved head, maybe twice your age, said something to you, and I reveled at how you shook him off. As if, right?

Had you lost weight? Tanned? Ah, it was the heels. I never saw you in heels. At one point, I second-guessed myself if it really was you. It's no wonder. I barely saw you in clothes other than your work uniform. Maybe we should've gone on actual dates. You were always working late. And who goes to brunch when they're under 30?

You weren't asking to marry me or even make things official. I never promised you this was going anywhere. We could resume on those terms. If you were interested.

Please be interested.

I took my eyes off of you to finish my drink and downgrade to beer. The chorus of a song played, but someone else found his way between us. I couldn't see your face anymore until you swayed a bit in laughter. Were you milking him for a freebie? I recommend the Manhattan.

When the two of you disappeared to a booth, I found myself no longer wanting to drink, yet emptying my glass right away leaving only foam. You must have seen me and given the chump a chance. Had you fallen so low as to give up a Saturday shift and accept a date?

I considered leaving. You'd see my exit and text me about it later.

I could text you right then, something like, "I was here first!"

You'd respond with, "Thanks for saying hi!" with a smiley or something. Enough to disrupt your conversation. What were you telling this man?

"No, I haven't been in anything serious in a while. Just casual." Or were you making yourself out to be a victim? Recruiting my substitute? I could almost hear you.

I was shaking. I needed someone near me to consult. I scanned the room for your replacement but saw no options. You weren't just the only attractive one in the bar, I hadn't encountered anyone near your beauty since I let you go. I closed my eyes for a moment and remembered everything about you. The little sounds you whispered in your sleep. That time we made ourselves late to our respective Easters. You certainly haven't forgotten. How often do those loops circulate in your mind?

And then you were both next to me. My glass nearly slipped from my hand. I wondered if you wanted me to save you.

Oddly enough, he spoke to me first. "Do you know if there's a band tonight?"

I couldn't look at you yet. "Are you two here to see one?" It was the perfect question.

"We're supposed to meet up with her folks in a bit, but they hate loud bars, so . . ."

I glanced at you, but you returned the look of a stranger I'd never met. "Yeah, probably not the best place to meet her parents for the first time," I said. If they left, I didn't have to go. I'd obliterate myself and get a cab home.

"No, it's cool," he said. "We've been together for two years. I know 'em well enough."

I saw you pull at his hand a bit. We looked at each other one last time before you turned away. You were indeed a stranger all along.

DEVIL'S RARE

Matt waited at the Lemp Mansion bar as the other groups arrived. The mirror behind the rows of liquor held a yellowish haze.

"We'll start our tour in about five minutes," a frumpy, older woman said.

Matt wished the bar was open. Some rare bourbons highlighted the back row of bottles. He glanced at the tour guide and stepped over to the bar's side to inspect further. He couldn't believe the selection: Blanton's, Stagg, and even a bottle of Pappy lined the wall. A small fortune to not be monitored. He gazed into the mirror at an angle to keep an eye on the tour group. Was it starting?

A rocks glass was within his reach. He cupped it and used his shirt to wipe the dust out. What was a little residue when it came to rare, vintage bourbon? Next to the popular bottles, he spotted another: Devil's Rare 18-Year, the label said. 18 years is a long time to be in a barrel only to be ignored in a bottle, Matt thought.

He waited, timed his moment, and then poured. No one noticed. They were over in the parlor now, hearing tales of the Lemp family members who ended their lives so early.

Nonsense, he thought, and then downed the rocks glass.

The word smooth wasn't justice. An immaculate caramel with hints of cooking spices and cinnamon blessed his palate. The heat reverberated through his nose and settled softly on his soul, hugging him like a warm blanket in the winter.

Another pour! Why not? The tour was now two rooms away.

Matt settled at the bar with his refill.

"I see you've helped yourself." A bartender appeared from seemingly nowhere. "Let me know when you're ready for another," the friendly man said. "They're on the house tonight."

Amazing! Matt thought. By his third drink, he was dying to know the story about the mirror.

"Nothing much," the bartender said. "We just think it looks classy. Could probably use a wipe-down."

Matt continued to stare into it. The yellow haze seemed to thicken.

Just then, he heard more voices. Uh-oh, busted. The guide would probably be insulted that he'd skipped her whole spiel. Matt kept his gaze forward, now seeing the familiar group of strangers in the mirror. He looked over his shoulder to accept his scolding.

They weren't behind him, but when he looked back into the mirror, the bar was crowded.

"And here we have our bar with its legendary and mysterious mirror."

Matt's stomach dropped. In the mirror, the people nearly touched him, but on his side of the reflection, he was alone, save for the bartender. Behind him, there were only walls. Where was the exit?

"And that concludes our tour," the woman said. Matt stared into the mirror, watching the crowd disperse.

"Wait," Matt said to the bartender. "When do I get to leave?"

"18 years is a long time," the bartender said.

NOT YET

I. The first time our paths crossed, all I noticed were her eyes. Hazel, like a cup of coffee with too much cream. They didn't seem to notice me, and I almost didn't notice them, but at the last moment before our routes intersected, I found myself starstruck by their hue.

II. It was a few days later. I'd nearly forgotten about her, but in almost the same spot, near the largest oak in the park, she passed by again. Her hair was tucked into an off-white hat, and a forest-green jacket covered her torso on that chilly late spring morning. Instantly, I recognized the memorable shade. I stared. It was as if my eyes were trying to say hello to hers, but there was no reply.

III. I admit I planned our encounter the following day. I'd taken note of our exact location and time, and though it happened further down the paved pathway, it still felt like a coincidence. I'm not sure if we made eye contact or not. I didn't want to be obvious, so I averted my gaze much earlier than the previous days. If I had to guess, I'd say she may have looked in my direction right before that split second when our bodies were exactly next to each other but facing opposite ways.

IV. I didn't see her this morning. Has it occurred to her that I glance her way every day? Would she be surprised to know it's the only part of my daily routine that I look forward to? She crosses my mind regularly now—while I'm waiting on copies or washing the dishes after dinner. At least she's motivated me to get my walk in every morning.

V. Today was perfect! I walked an extra lap around the park, but during round two, there she was. It was warmer, and she sported a white t-shirt with a yellow windbreaker tied around her waist. Light-gray sweatpants, you know, nothing super-coordinated. I don't think I'd want to be with someone who puts too much effort into their exercise wardrobe. I want someone who thinks like me, and I have reason to believe she might. We both seemed to notice each other from quite a distance, but then as we got closer, I watched her eyes look away, and for some reason, mine did too. We're a game of chicken where we both lose. Still, this game we play almost means more. I know my heart started to beat a little faster, and I felt like she knew me as a regular. Hopefully, I'm more than just an extra in her scenery. I'm excited for tomorrow.

VI. It's been almost a week, and I haven't seen her once. She disappeared as abruptly as she showed up. It's ridiculous how I find myself searching for her in other locations in our neighborhood. God, I spent twenty minutes in the bookstore. What kind of desperate, cliché loser have I become? It was only her eyes . . . not her personality. What if she loves K-pop and vampire movies? It would've never worked. There's a new girl at my office who isn't bad. Still, my walks have become lonely, monotonous disappointments instead of a positive, energizing exercise.

VII. I talked to the girl at work. Her name is Carol. She's an old soul, which is good because she's a few years younger than me. We all turn 30 eventually. Hopefully, she comes to the Friday happy hour where I'll try to sit down first and then see if she makes a point to sit near me. Or maybe I should wait and then sit near her? These aren't the questions I thought I'd be asking myself at this point in my life.

VIII. Guess who was back in the park today? The only reason I went was to think about my plans for happy hour. I confirmed that Carol was indeed going, and it's like my mystery woman knew I was thinking about someone else. Good news: She smiled at me today as we passed one another. The thing is, an old man walking his dog was right in front of me, which initiated her smile. The nod—yes, it was a full nod—was more of a reaction to both of us. It's not like she could just nod at the man and his pup and then ignore me. At least she's back in case things don't work out with Carol.

IX. I sat by Carol. Not at first, but when someone left early, she made her way over to chat with me. She talks a bit loud, but I think it was just because of the wine. Her teeth were stained purple, and she didn't get a lot of my references. I guess movies aren't her thing. We didn't exchange numbers, but it felt good to think about someone else. I don't expect Hazel Eyes to be in the park over the weekend. That's only happened once.

X. The oddest thing happened today! Hazel Eyes switched directions during her walk. She was there before I was, and I didn't notice her on my first lap, but when I stopped to check my phone, she walked past me from behind. Another smile too! I love how much more sunlight we're getting in the morning; it feels symbolic. So why did she switch directions? I wanted to follow her right away, but then what kind of creep trails a woman by a few feet her entire walk? I said the alphabet twice and then continued on my same path at a safe distance. I watched as she disappeared out of the park at the exit near the bus stop. I'm not sure if she rides the bus in and out of the neighborhood—I take it occasionally—but maybe we'll run into each other somewhere else.

XI. Carol asked me out. We're going to have dinner Friday. How do you like that? These younger girls breaking social norms. She was waiting by my Jeep after work (the fact that she knows what I drive!) and with the confidence of a homecoming queen asked if I'd like to hang out Friday night. It was a little intimidating, to be honest. I lied and told her I was thinking the same thing and that I would plan a fun night, and she was as happy as ever. We work on opposite sides of the office, so daily interaction is minimal, but that could change. I've got a date to prepare for!

XII. I should've known. The cute guy who always looks my way on our morning walks is taken. Desperate, I took the bus into town even on a Saturday morning and added two extra laps only to encounter him and some younger girl hand in hand. They were walking in the opposite direction of me, and of course, our encounter was at the narrowest part of the trail, so he had to step aside rather than release her hand to let me by. He looked shocked, like I'd caught him in an affair, but that's all in my head. We were never meant to be. She's why he never started a conversation. How many times can you cross paths with an attractive person and never make a move? Oh well, whoever she is, she's a lucky girl. Guess I'll try the bookstore.

HOW I GOT ON SPORTSCENTER

I noticed something about the fellas on our ballclub. When we nod to a teammate, our chin goes from low to high. When we nod to an opponent or maybe an ump, our chins go from high to low. That being said, after a series and a half in identical uniforms, we still nodded high to low to Blake Mondale . . . if we bothered to nod at all.

A major leaguer finishing up a rehab stint, Blake's five-year contract dwarfed us all. Hell, with his signing bonus, he could've bought all our homes, knocked them down, and rebuilt them twice as large. So you can imagine how stunned we were when Mr. Bigshot All-Star joined our postgame hang at this joint called The Frog-Bear after a 2-1 win over Columbus.

Most surprised was our right fielder, Chipper Flannigan. Me and Flanny were both Triple-A lifers. Now that I think about it, we've been teammates since before the guys in the clubhouse called him Flanny. A player has to be around a long time to replace a nickname like Chipper. Flanny's been called up to the big leagues half a dozen times, while I've only seen the bright lights twice. I've long since accepted the ceiling of my destiny, Flanny not so much.

So anyways, we're standing around the Frog-Bear pool tables, knocking back the local microbrew selection when the great Blake Mondale grabs a cue and calls "next" right as Flanny lines up a shot on the 8-ball. Without even a blink, Flanny buried the shot like a routine fly ball.

I should mention that Flanny specializes in two things: stealing bases and hustling chumps. So when Signing-Bonus-Baby Blake Mondale slapped down a C-note, Flanny made sure to lose the first game.

And the second.

And the third.

The rest of us gathered around because we knew this move better than a rookie's pickoff attempt. Flanny was setting Blake up like a pitcher sets up an inside fastball after a trio of sliders. Sure enough, the very next game, the hundreds scattered across the green felt. "One more game," Flanny said. "And let's make it a grand." Blue dust snowed as he ground the chalk against his cue.

"I don't know, man," Blake shifted his monstrous stature against the corner of the table. "I'm scheduled for a few more at-bats tomorrow, and then I gotta head back to the show pretty late."

That's all our games were to Blake: At-bats. Rehab. Batting practice. He showed no emotion whether we won or lost. He played on our squad just to get his timing back. By my count, he could've stretched a gap single into a double at least twice, but he would've had to slide on that precious rehabbed wrist. We weren't worth it. And forget about taking the field. Big Shot was just here to DH.

Flanny ignored Blake's attempt at an exit and racked the balls as the loose cash drew the eyes of outsiders.

Blake noticed the audience too. "Make it two grand." He smiled at us like we were allies.

"Twenty Benjamins it is," Flanny said, emptying his wallet.

Flanny broke and knocked a stripe in. His focus darted around the table, probably planning four shots ahead. "I'll take solids," he said. "You can have that fifteen." His next shot banked in the two-ball.

Then *she* walked over. We didn't get her name. We didn't need her name. She was in every city. Thirty-something dressed like twenty-something. Or twenty-something dressed like she wasn't old enough to drink. Blonde, brunette, redhead, older, younger, dangerously younger, show-me-your-ID younger, Flanny was game. She eyed both men but smiled at the stack of cash sitting atop the corner pocket as Flanny drained three straight balls into it.

By the time Blake got off his stool to approach the cue ball, he knew he'd been sharked. He gave the gal an up-and-down, but she was charmed by Flanny and the cash. Two crafty bank shots allowed Blake to salvage a little dignity, but Flanny quickly finished off the 8-ball with a behind-the-back shot that had his newest fan giggling like a schoolgirl.

"That'll make Sportscenter tonight," our catcher Chops said.

Instinctively, we all looked up at the television as a familiar face appeared in the graphic behind the anchorman. "The Yankees expect Blake Mondale back as soon as this weekend as he finishes rehabbing his broken wrist in the minors. Scranton finishes a series with a day game in Columbus tomorrow where Mondale will take his final few at-bats before returning to the Bronx."

I thought the broad's head was gonna snap off the way she looked back and forth from the TV to the man in front of her. And Flanny? He was just a discarded towel on the clubhouse floor.

Blake owned the room again, like a big brother taking over his little brother's treehouse.

It didn't even require eye contact. Blake adjusted his gold Rolex, which may as well have been the dangling pocket watch of a hypnotist. "You ready to get outta here?" he said in the gal's direction.

When she nodded yes, he still wasn't looking. He didn't have to. They disappeared arm in arm while poor Flanny stood there looking as dumb as the victim of the hidden-ball trick. Even the fistful of cash didn't save his pride.

***

Giving Flanny a whole night to plot his revenge is like a pitcher allowing a ten-foot lead-off without throwing over. All game, I could tell he was still sore about the night before, but he was taking it out on the opponents. Heading into the sixth inning, he was already three-for-four, including a triple. Columbus was on their fifth pitcher while we all batted around for the second straight inning.

I saw Blake approach our manager, so I listened in.

"I'll take one more at-bat, but give me a pinch runner if it stays in the park." Just like with his groupie from last night, he didn't bother to make eye contact. He just told Skipper how it was.

None of us dared to command our manager like this, but then again, none of us would be wearing the trademark pinstripes in the Bronx that weekend.

Flanny led the inning off with a single to short left, and it appeared we were on our way to another crooked number while already up eleven runs. Chops and Billy both flew out to deep right before it was Blake's turn to hit. It was evident this at-bat was the only reason Columbus fans were still in the park. Maybe he'd send a souvenir to the left-field seats.

Blake intended to make the most of this final big-fish-in-a-small-pond adventure and took his sweet time strutting from the on-deck circle to the batter's box. I could've sworn I saw the pitcher look at an imaginary wristwatch as Blake dug in.

The kid on the mound went into his stretch, and Flanny took a lead the size of Texas.

"Uh oh," I mumbled. I had a hunch of his scheme.

"Is he trying to get picked off?" our skipper groaned. A pickoff would rob Blake of his final at-bat . . . or keep him around another inning. A small thorn in the star's side for the previous night's humiliation.

I shook my head no. Flanny had much worse in store for our stud.

The pitcher tossed over to first, but Flanny raced back without a slide.

Blake stepped out of the box and looked back at us like we had answers.

The pitcher gathered himself and peered at the catcher's signal once more. Every single man in the dugout knew what pitch was coming. High and tight. Sure enough, Blake stumbled backward out of the box, glaring. As the pitcher walked back to pick up the rosin bag, we realized Blake's scowl was on Flanny instead of the man who threatened to take his chin off.

Flanny took another huge lead at the 1-0 count, but this time as the pitcher delivered a fastball, he took off towards second.

I'll admit, the crack of the bat from Blake Mondale sounds different than the rest of ours. Like it's got a microphone next to it. He sent the ball a mile toward the horizon, but foul. It might have landed two neighborhoods over. Meanwhile, Flanny stood on second base before trotting back to first.

Now both teams knew the ploy. Hell, I'd guess even most of the fans suspected. Flanny, the crazy son-of-a-bitch, was violating one of baseball's sacred, unwritten rules by attempting to steal a base with a double-digit lead. The scapegoat of this penalty stood at the plate armed only with a bat and a plastic helmet.

A smirk slipped from Flanny's face. He took another massive lead. The pitcher threw over once more while Blake shot a few more daggers from the batter's box.

Our rather pugnacious dugout rose to its feet now, ready for the ensuing brawl once Blake got beamed. "Here we go again," I heard Chops mumble.

The pitcher quickly went to his stretch. No signal was needed for this pitch. The only question was how high he was going to throw it.

Most of us were to the dugout steps by the time he unloaded what had to be a hundred-mile-an-hour fastball that split Mondale's shoulder blades with a thud. He grimaced, slammed his bat down, and sprinted towards the mound like a madman. The poor pitcher put up his dukes and stutter-stepped towards his dugout. But here's when we all got a dose of surprise. Blake Mondale sprinted right past the opposing pitcher and continued towards the instigator of this chaos, his teammate Chipper Flannigan. Ol' Flanny didn't stand a chance as Blake pounded him into the ground. As a squad, we didn't know whether to break it up, or let nature run its course. I ran up to the scrum and got as close as I could, and for the first time in my baseball career, I saw myself on SportsCenter that night. Unfortunately, none of the gals at the bar noticed.

Part 4

"Remainders of a shooting star
Landed directly on our broke down little car
Before then, we had made a wish
That we would be missed
If one or another just did not exist"

Little Motel
by Modest Mouse

This next section is the least autobiographical but spans an entire spectrum of emotions. "Best Friend" takes place in a community much like the one I grew up in. "Dog Named Blue" is a change of pace based on a Father John Misty song called "Goodbye Mr. Blue." "Brain Cooks Heart" is another flash fiction involving infatuation. "The Seven Gates of Hell" was written after I learned of a local urban myth. They say anyone who drives under the seven railroad bridges in a certain order in Collinsville, Illinois can visit Hell if they cross the final one at midnight.

BEST FRIEND

I just wanted to watch the Bears game and sip beer. Charlie had a different motive: a strawberry-blonde bartender. The bar located in his little town was dirt cheap with prices comparable to back in the Bears' glory days.

"Just say things that make me sound cool," Charlie said. "Her name's Mandy and you'll see how much she flirts with me."

"Gotcha," I said. I texted my father about the Bears being favored in their game then pocketed my phone. Charlie would need all my attention.

We had our choice of seats as it was still ten minutes before noon kickoff. Neither the jukebox nor the Pac-Man machine was turned on yet. The dartboard was pockmarked with pores. An old man at the furthest barstool turned and peered at us as we sat at two stools towards the middle, near the beer taps.

Charlie fiddled with his hands and looked around. "She's here. Probably in the back."

I didn't doubt it. There was nothing else going on in this civilization.

"There!" He punched my shoulder as if I needed prompting about the only living thing (aside from the dinosaur who was still staring at us) in the joint.

Mandy looked . . . local, and way different than her heavily filtered online pictures Charlie insisted I thumb through on the drive over. For one, she wasn't as shiny.

She sounded really happy. "Hi, Charlie! Who's this?"

Charlie stood and almost knocked his barstool over. "Mandy, this is Greg. Really close buddy of mine."

She stuck her hand out to shake over the bar, so I obliged. Then she leaned over a bit in what I like to call a cleavage flex. Honestly, her pose wasn't doing it for me. Her hair had that crunchy hold to it, and her shirt was two sizes too small. One of her cuspids that looked darker and crooked intruded her smile. There are no photo filters in real life. But hey, this gave Charlie a realistic shot, I figured. All I had to do was occasionally coach my pal and drink for under twenty bucks while watching football.

By the middle of the first quarter, a handful of regulars sat near us. I worried we'd taken their usual seats. I overheard a lot of conversations that began with phrases like, "I seen . . ." and "We was . . ." I kept my judgment to myself and was proud of Charlie's progress. He'd made Mandy laugh twice already.

When his dream girl went to the walk-in cooler he asked, "Isn't she great?"

"Yeah, she's got quite a laugh," I said.

"Her body though, right? I mean, what a dime."

I nodded and finished my second beer. Since I wasn't driving us and the game was already going awry, getting drunk felt inevitable. I could crash at Charlie's place instead of heading back into the city. He'd love that.

Mandy came back and looked up at the television. "Ugh! Not going well, is it?"

"That's why I'm a Packers fan," Charlie said. He always had been. There was no geographical logic to it. He didn't know much about football anyway, so I let him have his fun to an extent. "Can we watch them instead?"

"They play Monday night," I said. Some fan, right?

"I don't have to work Monday night," Mandy said. She was looking up at the TV again, so I glanced at Charlie. It took my eyebrows and a head bob before he realized that was a hint.

"Should I?" he mouthed.

I shook my head quickly. "Not yet."

Mandy poured another round of scotch for the old man and chatted him up for a bit.

"Wait until we're about to leave," I said. "Otherwise, it'll be awkward whether she accepts or not."

"Can you ask her if she'd say yes while I go to the—"

"No, this isn't middle school. She'll say yes."

"Fine, but where do I take her?" He twisted his mouth. "There's an Olive Garden in the next town."

I looked around. "That works."

"You don't think it's too fancy for a first date?"

Now you understand the patience I had to have with a friend like Charlie.

"Trust me, it's not," I said. Charlie gave a double fist pump under the bar before Mandy returned her attention to us.

"There's a Fireball special," she said. "Two for three bucks." She held the bottle and jiggled it playfully.

"What do you say, Greg?"

"Fire away," I said. "Unless you want to give Mandy the other shot."

"Oh no, Sweetie," she said. "Hair of the dog doesn't work on me."

After we did our shots, the venue got even busier. Mandy scrambled, mixing well drinks and opening beer bottles with one swipe. I noticed Charlie's silence.

"You okay there, buddy?"

"It's just . . . Why did she call *you* Sweetie?"

"That's what bartenders and waitresses do. Everyone is a sweetie. That old man with no teeth is a sweetie. The cockroach in the bathroom is a sweetie."

"I'm not."

"Because she would mean it with you, or you get some other nickname beyond Sweetie."

Charlie nodded. "How'd you get so smart about girls?"

He was way too loud. Maybe I'd have to drive after all. I didn't want to try and explain anything during the Bears' two-minute drill. They had a chance to cut the lead to single digits.

"Just a gut feeling," I said. "You'll learn their tricks eventually."

"That's why you're my best friend," he said.

"Dude," I said. I didn't want to be forced into any reciprocation. There were a half-dozen guys and a handful of girls off the top of my head who I was closer with than Charlie.

"Sorry, sorry!" Charlie laughed. "Mandy, can we get two more Fireballs?"

This time I slapped down a five and waved away the change. Drinks were going down smoothly, but certainly, there wasn't an Uber or Lyft for miles.

Charlie could tell what I was thinking. "Relax, I know the cop well enough. He's cool, plus it's not too far. I'll get us home."

After halftime, the aforementioned cop showed up. Charlie was on his feet immediately. "Ralph, come meet my friend Greg."

I found myself shaking the hand of a man with a badge, gun, and crew cut. "I've heard a lot about you, Greg. Nice to finally put a name to the face."

Why?

"Ralph, tell him about the guy who was going 120 last week." Charlie sounded like a little boy.

Ralph stretched a small anecdote into a ten-minute story with at least two racial slurs that no one but me flinched at. The tale dripped with embellishment. There were three different times I thought the story had ended, only to have my arm tapped—no, pounded—by Charlie to make sure I was paying close enough attention. "Check this part out," he kept saying as if I had a choice.

By the time the "Legend of the Black Camaro" ended, the Bears were down by three touchdowns. I was buzzing, but not drunk. It was stuffy inside, and someone was smoking a cigarette that didn't seem to bother anyone else. When the door opened, sunlight from a beautiful autumn day leaked into our dark, moldy habitat. Another beer appeared in front of me, courtesy of the departing cop. Charlie seemed to be holding Mandy's attention fairly well, considering how busy she was. She'd laugh and make flirty faces with him and even touched his hand for a few seconds, saying she'd "be right back."

"Can I drink this outside?" I asked Charlie.

"Why?"

"Need a little air. The game's gotten ugly, and it looks nice out."

"You don't want to leave already, do you? You said you wanted to watch the whole game."

I'd said that to make sure we didn't abandon an exciting finish, which was now a snowball's chance. There was a man behind the bar now. Charlie explained he was Mandy's boss and nobody liked him very much because of his political rants.

I didn't care. "Sir, can we drink outside?"

He looked offended at first, but then I repeated myself.

"Oh, yeah. I closed the patio down after Labor Day, but if you need to smoke . . . Just don't break that bottle, or me and you are gonna have a problem."

Confused by the hostility, I grabbed my beer and carried it through the exit. I squinted into the sunlight, but it felt good to smell anything other than the bar haze.

Four weathered picnic tables lined the back, their light blue paint peeling. I sat atop one and considered my options. I could get drunk enough to try and fit in with my surroundings just this once. Or I could tell Charlie we should leave and that he should ask Mandy out for tomorrow night. I knew she'd say yes.

A burst of laughter leaked from the bar as a back door I hadn't noticed opened up. It was Mandy and the naval that peaked from above her belt buckle.

"Soberin' up?" she asked.

"Hopefully."

"Got any smokes?" The table adjusted as she sat next to me.

"Sorry, I don't partake."

"I shouldn't neither."

It was my turn, I guess. "So, Charlie. I think he really likes you."

"Yeah, he's a super great guy. I've had my eye on him for a while, but before today, he hardly said much."

"You're welcome," I said. We both laughed.

Right then, Mandy pressed her hand on my cheek and turned it, and we were kissing. I almost laughed, but she was pretty good at it. I finally pulled away.

She rested her arm against mine. I could feel the warmth of her skin. "I live right over there." She pointed at a small yellow house across the street and a block down. "It's my lunch break technically."

I looked up at the backdoor, then down at my shoes.

"I know what you're thinking," she said. "If she's that good of a kisser . . ."

I thought back to my sophomore year about a girl way out of my league who blessed me with a night in her dorm room.

"No, but thank you," I said. I looked her in the eyes like I was simply declining another beer.

"I didn't think so, but you was worth a shot." She bumped her shoulder against mine like we were buddies.

I nodded slowly, flattered.

"Well, I should get back in there." She hopped up and disappeared through the back door.

I didn't stay outside much longer. I emptied my beer too quickly and needed to pee. Back inside, the game had been changed to NASCAR, and Charlie was playing pool against a stranger.

"He bet me ten bucks, and I'm killing him," Charlie whisper-yelled into my ear.

"You're getting hustled," I said. "Don't play a second game, no matter what. We should get going."

His eyes widened. "Dude, you're so smart!"

He sank the 8-ball and got called a "stupid homo" for declining a rematch.

"Told ya," I said.

He nodded and wobbled a bit. "Thanks for being my best friend," he said. His voice cracked and his eyes glistened.

"Any time. Now go ask Mandy out."

DOG NAMED BLUE

I can't say I would've shown up to Blue's burial had he died six months earlier, around when Wendy and I had last spoken. Our mutt, the one we adopted years ago as a lovable puppy, lay ice-cold in a silver Hefty bag.

The overnight cold front was a shock to everyone. The flurries started to collect on the small mound of dirt as Wendy shivered next to me. "My dad dug the hole yesterday."

I nodded and should've asked how her dad was doing—I missed him after the breakup too—but I was still balancing the emotion from not seeing her in so long. And then Blue's body in that bag. "That was kind of him." I finally turned to her. "Tell him I said hello."

She tilted her head. The cold was an excuse for both of us to stay wrapped up in our coats, gloved hands buried in our pockets, so different from the way we were. Our friends used to mock our attached hands. In line, in the car, and anywhere on foot, we were an unbreakable red rover wall, swinging in laughter back then.

She spoke again. "This is kind of a weird question, but did you want to see him one last time? I mean, I told him goodbye the day we had to do this, but I didn't know . . ."

A choke I disguised as a laugh slipped from me. "Remember the first time we brought him out to this field? He'd never seen so much space."

The wind picked up, and now Wendy seemed to be fighting a lump in her throat too. "He was so happy back then."

We all were. Our relationship was as fresh as the first week of June. Before sunburn and before the songs of the summer grow tiresome. She was my first love, and I never thought the shadows would angle themselves any differently. But June turns to July, July to August, and August to September. The amusement parks close, the lake water cools, and the docks become vacant. It doesn't happen all at once. You feel it slipping away like the tan on your summer skin. I tried to prevent it, but no one is immune to time as feelings fade.

That's what happened to us, and in a desperate rationalization, I let her keep Blue, thinking I was just lending him while I moved on from our relationship.

The flakes halted, but the wind held steady. It cut through the denim of my jeans, but I didn't care. I'm not sure how much time passed before she finally broke another accidental silence.

"Are you still seeing someone?"

I shook my head no. Earlier in the year, I told myself I was in love and that Wendy and Blue no longer mattered in my life. I'd even declined temporary custody of my former dog while Wendy traveled with her new boyfriend.

"Remember the time," I said, "he got himself buried in the sheets and tore the covers off of the entire bed?" The story allowed me to feign a little joy.

"And then he fell off the bed and was still stuck."

The laughter felt warming. The tension deflated, and we edged towards facing one another. I recalled the way I freed Blue's head from the sheets that wonderful morning as I took his face in my hands. Suddenly, I knelt to the bag and pulled the strings open. His eyes and mouth were shut tightly, frozen by death and winter.

When was the last time I'd seen those eyes? How could I have known they'd never look at me again? I regretted that I could not remember my last walk with Blue. The last time I'd flipped a treat he would catch in mid-air. And this would be the last time I would rub my thumbs across his narrow face.

Had he died six months ago, I wouldn't have trusted myself around Wendy and would have missed this moment. Ironically enough, she was the one in a relationship now, so there was nothing I could do.

I didn't hear the new voice right away or even turn to look, but as her new partner approached, I gathered he was on a phone call. I stayed on my knees, knowing that as soon as I chose, it would be the last time I saw Blue's face.

"Okay," the new voice said, "so we're trying to change the reservation to 8:30 so we can hang with her parents for a little bit, but I'll let you know."

The insensitive intruder loomed over me, his faint shadow covering Blue's grave. I stood up. My knees and legs felt 70 years old now.

"Kevin, this is Peter. He's the one I was telling you about that lived with me and Blue."

I grimaced at the unshaven face of the man still on his phone.

"I'll just text you. It'll either be 7:30 or 8:30 depending on what the restaurant can do . . . Yeah, he still works there, but he can't pull that big of a string . . . Okay, I gotta go. What?" Kevin finished his phone call with laughter that dug into my chest. "Babe, you took him back out of the bag? Kinda gross, right?"

I inhaled deeply and let the frigid air bite my lungs. When I released it, my breath lingered in front of me. "I wanted to see him one last time." I didn't look at Kevin. "He was mine too."

"Oh, that's cool." Kevin lit a cigarette and stood silently except for the long exhale of his first drag. The stench penetrated the moment. The snow resumed slightly heavier, pitter-pattering on the bag.

"Honey, maybe go wait in the car?" Wendy said. "I'll just be another minute or two."

Kevin obeyed the way I used to. Wendy wasn't someone you said no to very often.

As Kevin walked away, the tears suddenly spilled from my eyes, melting the fresh flakes on the bag. I pulled the strings, covering my little buddy once and for all. Wendy was mumbling something about her dad not leaving the shovel, but he'd be out later to cover Blue for us.

"This is the last time, isn't it?" I asked.

"You can always come visit. Dad would understand why you're in his field."

"No, I mean us. This is the last time I'll see you."

"Oh."

"I didn't realize I'd never see Blue again, and maybe that made it easier to leave him, but now I'm realizing . . ."

"Sometimes the last time comes too soon." She reached out and squeezed my hand, then turned and walked back towards the road where our cars were parked.

With the same hand she'd squeezed, I picked up a fistful of dirt and dropped it on my buddy.

BRAIN COOKS HEART

Albert entered the detention room, squinting as if the lights themselves were part of the punishment.

"Not a peep," Mr. Johnson told the boys in front. They had their hoods pulled up, so Albert felt safe from their peripheral.

Jennifer entered moments later. He'd failed to train himself not to stare. He tried to guide her to the closest seat using the telepathy methods he loved in his favorite sci-fi series, but alas, she favored three desks over. She'd seen him and made a conscious decision to sit at a desk in *his* row. They were stars in the same constellation.

When she looked over, he let his head drop to a blank sheet of paper. His prop. He got out a pen and began the outline of a starship. Jennifer's focus changed to the clock above the door. Finally, some time to gaze at her red hair. The pattern of freckles on the back of her arm. The pale white below her leggings just above her ankles. How warm was her skin today?

Once, during a fire drill on the way back into the building, he'd brushed against her. Her woolly sweater made his arm itch, but he didn't scratch it, choosing instead to revel in the contact and its aftermath.

"Austin, Caleb, TJ," Mr. Johnson read off his clipboard. "I know why you're here." They played with the strings on their hoodies. "Jennifer?"

"I was late to class again," she said.

Albert drew in his breath at this. What made her late? A broken traffic light? A sibling? He exhaled steam at the thought it had something to do with a guy. The teacher continued his round of persecution as Albert suddenly realized he had no story.

"Who are you?"

"Albert."

"Al-bert . . . Al-bert. I don't even see you on my list."

His face reddened, and he looked at his paper. The exhaust from the starship on his paper had no answers. One of the hooded faces turned with a snicker.

"I . . ."

"He's here because of me," Jennifer said.

His ears rang in terror. How did she know? The fire in his cheeks burned until sweat appeared on his forehead.

"Because of you," Mr. Johnson stated.

"I made him late to class too." She folded her arms and leaned back like she'd executed a magic trick.

The teacher shrugged and returned to his desk.

The heat subsided, but a different warmth grew within. They worked as a team. Maybe there was indeed telepathy between them. He'd earned it from months and months of thinking of her every night. Somehow, their brains had connected. Next, their hearts.

He waited a moment before looking back over to her. Another message to her brain: Give me a sign you can hear me.

Jennifer slowly turned her head, careful that no one else

saw. Her lips moved, and though the words were never vocalized, the message was clear. "Stop following me."

THE SEVEN GATES
OF HELL

"This is taking, like, forever. What a stupid idea," Jill complained from the backseat. "How much longer? I'm not getting grounded for this, you know."

Brad exhaled with frustration. "You insisted on coming along, Sunshine."

"I know, but it's just . . . so freaking stupid."

Murphy sighed and looked over at his friend. "Stop it, you two. We have eight and a half minutes to get to the last gate."

The first six gates, graffitied railroad bridges that were overpasses, had been simple enough to drive through. The three teens had scouted the route the previous week, only to quit before reaching the final overpass that supposedly led to Hell if crossed at midnight. A few classmates had tried, but no one claimed to have pulled off the perfect timing. The "Portal to Hell" needed an exact order of gates and perfect timing. Murphy and Brad had made it their mission to disprove the legend, and this time, they were determined to make it through all seven gates.

"Are you sure we have enough gas?" Jill asked, her hand gripping Brad's shoulder.

"We aren't using that excuse again," Murphy said.

"Until you chip in, you've got no say in it." Brad flicked on the high beams, and the three rode in silence until the female voice on the GPS announced, "Rerouting."

"Shit, not again," Murphy groaned, pulling out his phone. "We should be okay. I think we just stay on this road until it forks, then hang a right. After that, the bridge is down a hill."

"We should've practiced in the daytime," Jill said.

"Practiced?" Brad scoffed.

"You're just scared," Murphy said, not bothering to look back at her. "Take another sip of courage."

"I could go for one," Brad admitted.

"No way!" Jill snatched the bottle from his lips. "You don't get—"

Brad slammed on the brakes. The car skidded on the dirt road.

"Dammit, Brad!" Jill yelled. "I spilled all down my front, and now my parents are gonna smell it when I get home."

"If," Murphy said, turning on the dome light. "If, you get home." The boys laughed as Jill pounded Brad's shoulder.

"Relax, it'll dry. And besides, if we're heading into Hell, no one's gonna notice a little whiskey."

"I don't know, Brad. She might catch on fire. That stuff was hundred-proof."

"Neither of you are funny."

Murphy clicked the light off and heard Jill guzzle the last of the bottle. The brief silence was refreshing.

"Here's the fork," Brad said.

"Next stop, Hell."

"I—" Jill began.

"What?"

"I think I have to pee."

"I think we're already in hell," Murphy said.

Brad let out a sigh. "What do you want me to do, pull over?"

"Uh, yeah." Jill unbuckled her seatbelt.

"We have three minutes. Can't you pee after we get to Hell?"

"You're such a jerk! Why can't you be a gentleman for once in your life?"

"Why can't you be anything but a baby?"

"Well, I'm already soaked in liquor, I may as well just piss all over the backseat like one."

Her shrill voice grated on Murphy's nerves. It always seemed to go like this. Why did he even hang out with these two? It was torturous. He pressed his hand against his throbbing temple.

"Fine, fine," said Brad. He hit the brake again, and she hopped out. She disappeared behind the red brake lights.

"I gotta drop her," Brad said.

"No shit," said Murphy. "She ruins everything."

Brad lowered the window. "Hurry up!"

Still wiping her shirt, Jill climbed back into the car.

"OK, eight-tenths of a mile and we've got less than a minute until midnight," Brad said. The car rumbled down a hill. Rocks popped from beneath the tires. Murphy could hear Jill sobbing in the back. His friendship with Brad was so much better before she was in the picture. Now almost every night out ended in a fight. How had his buddy put up with her this long?

"I think that's it," Brad said, letting the car coast at a slower speed.

"Aaand, it's midnight. Go!" Murphy said. Jill continued

to whimper in the back.

The headlights shone on the graffiti that surrounded the passage. Unsymmetrical pentagrams and sixes decorated the archway. The headlights thinned. The road smoothed out.

At midnight, at exactly 31 miles per hour, the car and the three teens entered and exited the seventh gate of Hell.

"Oh my god, nothing even happened," Jill said. "I told you."

"I felt something," said Brad.

Murphy shrugged.

"What a waste," said Jill. "You guys are so stupid. I can't believe we wasted a Saturday and a half tank of gas, not to mention the liquor you made me spill. God, get me home already." Murphy closed his eyes, hoping she'd finally shut up.

When he opened them it felt much later.

"This is taking, like, forever. What a stupid idea," Jill complained from the backseat. "How much longer? I'm not getting grounded for this, you know."

Brad exhaled with frustration. "You insisted on coming along, Sunshine."

"I know, but it's just . . . so freaking stupid."

Part 5

"Whenever I breathe in,
You're breathing out"

*Whenever I Breathe Out, You Breathe In
(Positive/Negative)
by Modest Mouse*

"Once a Year" might be my favorite story in this collection. It's about a comedian who puts himself in a very tough position. It's balanced by two shorter works including "Top Shelf" featuring my favorite fictional liquor, Devil's Rare, yet again, and then one titled "The Turn" about my favorite person to golf with: my father. The last story titled, "The One with Sex in It" has the potential to be the first chapter of my next novel.

ONCE A YEAR

For the fourth straight year, Clint Keller's tour schedule took him through the "Laugh It Up" Comedy Club in Fayetteville, Arkansas. And for the fourth straight year, Kyla Brown waited on him after the show.

The first year, when she was a sophomore at Arkansas waiting tables, and he was a young man suffering from a recent heartbreak, they discovered one another after the club's poker game.

The second year, despite Kyla's boyfriend, whom she proudly displayed all over her Instagram account, they connected with the intensity of newlyweds.

The third year, they spent two days (and nights) together and Clint even canceled a low-paying gig to stick around for another 24 hours.

The other 51 weeks of the year, they lived like distant satellites, without so much as a birthday text. Clint imagined Kyla got as jealous as he did whenever a new apparent partner showed up in online pictures.

It was a given Kyla would be around that night when he entered the club, though she'd graduated and traded in waiting tables to become a third-grade teacher. Clint's career had also evolved. He was now the headliner instead of a middle act, and now it was his name on the marquee.

Aside from their professional upgrades, there was something else different this time. Clint was in love back in Iowa. Maybe Kyla would spare him some charm once he told her.

His set went well. An almost sold-out room of 250 loved his take on 80s movies, driving in the South, and the local references he secretly made in every city. As a bonus, he sold three dozen t-shirts while the club manager patted him on the back. It wasn't until the lobby was almost empty that he thought about Kyla. And then she appeared.

A short white skirt, tan shoulders, and a smile that could resolve the conflict in the Middle East approached him. As they embraced, the smell on her neck triggered images of their last passionate encounter. She pressed a cheek against his and then stepped back.

"I wore these wedges so I could be taller."

"Ah, I thought something was different." He took her all in. "And your hair too. It's lighter."

"Yeah, a little. Glad you noticed."

Clint looked around. The bartender had dimmed all the lights and abandoned his post. The club wasn't going to host this rendezvous.

"Follow me," Kyla said.

Before Clint could say anything, she was striding out to the parking lot. Clint retrieved his duffle bag of t-shirts from his sales table and followed. Catching up over a drink was harmless. Kyla would understand his situation and respect it once he explained.

The air outside was still warm. "There's a new bar we can hit," she said. "It just opened so none of the college kids know about it yet. Follow my car."

Clint wondered if she suspected his relationship. She seemed hurried and terse as if she could build momentum to get what she wanted. It allowed his inner voice to repeat that he'd done nothing wrong.

After a short drive to the adjacent neighborhood, they parked a row apart. The lot was dark, but out-of-season Christmas lights decorated "Drummer's Place." Clint's stomach twisted inside as he exited his car.

"See?" Kyla said. "No one's here! We're trying to spread the rumor to the undergrads that it's a gay bar, but the owner won't hang a rainbow up."

Clint paused again to tell her, but instead, she grabbed his hand and led him to the door. Maybe his body language would hint that this wasn't like previous years. When he loosened his grip she squeezed harder.

Yep, Kyla knew exactly what she was doing. She stopped talking for the first time and let him feel his hand in hers. The silence screamed her thoughts. *She doesn't matter because you are mine. You know what you want.*

Inside, a speaker blasted to a nearly empty room. "I'll get the first round," Clint said. He had to control something, even if it weakened his cause. He then realized by saying "first" he'd committed to having more than one round.

"I'll find us a table," Kyla said, walking away. "You know what I like."

Clint cringed. "A Black Russian for her, and a Bud Light for me." Beer was safe. A twenty from his t-shirt sales paid for the drinks and yielded a large tip.

On his way to the high-top table, he noticed how many other guys stared at Kyla. A sense of pride took over as he sat across from her. She thanked him and then leaned forward to talk. "Why is it so loud in here?"

He didn't have an answer but liked how the music seemed to come between them. "It's okay. I'm used to it," he said.

"Well, I'm not." She slid her bar stool right next to his.

"I have to tell you something," he said.

Right then, Kyla's phone buzzed on the table. She turned it face up, not even trying to hide the text. "Sorry, I'm seeing someone, just a sec." She thumbed a quick message, and for the first time, Clint relaxed a bit. Now would be the perfect time. "He treats me well, but it's still new, so I'm hoping it goes somewhere."

Clint knew how bad his poker face was, but tried to smother his jealousy. "I'm seeing someone too," he said.

"Oh, do you need to text her? Go ahead."

So much for control. She'd reduced his relationship like it was a weather report.

"We're pretty serious actually," he said.

"Uh-huh." Kyla was typing on her phone again and didn't look up. "What's her name?"

Clint took an extra second and his eyes looked up to the ceiling. "MaryAnn."

Kyla laughed. "Are you sure?"

"Sometimes she goes by just Mary, and I call her—"

"Sure! Sounds like you're tight." She continued to laugh.

Why had it taken him so long to produce her name? He had to counter. "What's your boyfriend's name?"

"Now you're gonna laugh at me." She pressed two fingers on his arm and then withdrew them.

"Then we're even. Come on, spit it out."

She sipped her drink. "Chad."

Clint pressed his lips together. They'd joked about guys named Chad during their previous encounters. Somehow, her boyfriend's name spawned memories of the lazy mornings she'd rest on his chest. Clint guessed she was remembering those mornings too, after the candles melted away and neither wanted to ever let go of the other.

He considered getting up and leaving her there, but he knew he couldn't. What if MaryAnn didn't work out? He couldn't burn a bridge with Kyla. And there it was, the doubt in his current relationship. While Kyla babbled about all the sweet things Chad did to woo her, Clint pondered the last five months with his girlfriend. Had MaryAnn ever cheated on him or was the love mutual? Then he reminded himself he hadn't done anything wrong. He would stop at one drink and send Kyla back to Chad while doing his best to battle jealousy.

Chad must have texted again because Kyla grew annoyed with her phone. "Sorry, I can't decide if he's clingy or sweet."

"Well, it is a Friday night. I wouldn't let you out of my sight." He instantly regretted his statement.

Somehow, Kyla didn't acknowledge the remark. Clint knew he should've felt relieved, but now Kyla was smiling as she typed. She wasn't as dangerous as he thought.

Just then, the bartender walked up. "Not closing just yet, but it's last call."

Clint signaled for another round for both of them right as Kyla slid some cash out to pay. As the bartender left to retrieve their drinks, she held up her phone to take a selfie. "Sorry, I know, I know."

Clint resisted the urge to mock her and drummed his fingers on the table. There had to be something to talk about that didn't drain into a flow chart leading back to their incredible sexual history.

"So you're . . . happy then?" Kyla asked.

"Yeah, I'm starting to headline more and more clubs,

and I've even turned down a few gigs. I upgraded my apartment, ditched my shitty roommate, replaced my car finally."

"Interesting," said Kyla.

"What?" But the bartender dropped off their drinks. And shots.

"You two are the only good tippers tonight. I hope these are okay." The bonus drinks were light yellow. Something with citrus. "They're called lemon drops."

They waited until he left to burst out laughing. Kyla went first. "Oh wow, sir. I've never heard of a lemon drop. So exotic."

Clint loved her laugh. Back when she waited tables at the comedy club, he could hear hers separate from the crowd and often caught himself directing his material to wherever she was in the room. "I guess we look like sorority sisters," he said. They laughed a little longer before taking the shots. "So what were you saying?"

"I just asked if you were happy, and you told me about your job and apartment and car."

Clint shrugged. "I'm happy with MaryAnn too."

"Good, 'cause I'm not cheating on Chad with you." She laughed again and then flashed a sexy photo-shoot grin.

So that was it. The past was the past for her too. Clint absorbed it and wasn't sure if he believed her. If he pulled her into the hallway by the restrooms or if they went to their cars, he could definitely change her mind. Still, it was an ease on his conscience for the relentless attraction he felt for her. He remembered thinking last time they were naked together he'd never see a waist-to-hip ratio like hers again. She was prettier than MaryAnn but in a different way. She was the kind of hot that guys know you don't get to date unless you're wealthy. MaryAnn and her long legs were taller but—why hold this disgusting comparison?

"Clint? Hello? Was it something I said?"

The music was still too loud. "Sorry, I think that venomous lemon drop is kicking in."

Kyla shook her head and looked like he'd disappointed her. He still craved her approval. "Did you want another one?"

"The lemon drop? No. Get me something real this time."

Clint walked to the bar, fishing another twenty from his wallet. This was a test . . . or a trap. If he got her something like a tequila, his intentions would be transparent. Whiskey? Even more direct. But he reminded himself that she stated (and she'd done it first) that she wasn't going to cheat on a guy named Chad. Maybe it was her way of avoiding possible rejection.

Clint was still unsure of his order when he got to the bar. Almost everyone else had cleared out, and the bartender faced him with a perturbed look.

"Sorry, I know you said last call, but . . ." He slid the twenty in front of him. "Can I get a shot of Grey Goose and a shot of Patron?" He'd let her decide. Either was fine with him.

Back at the table, Kyla smiled as she rested her chin on her hand. "What did you do? What did you do, you naughty boy?"

"I wasn't sure what to get you, so it's a choose-your-own-adventure. Vodka or tequila." He slid both to the middle of the table.

"So symbolic," Kyla said. "One is a crisp, classy liquor that makes martinis." She rotated the glass a couple of times, stuck her finger in it, and tasted it. "The other is a party that starts innocent enough, but then transforms you into your alter-ego." She finger-tasted the other as well. "Ooh, top shelf."

Intrigued by where this analogy was going, Clint stayed quiet.

"So the question is, which one am I?" She tilted her head. "And which one is MaryKate?"

Clint didn't correct her and instead noticed his heart was beating much faster. This little act erased the platonic statements from earlier. "Which do you want to be?" he said.

Kyla stared into his eyes for a moment, letting him dig himself deeper into a forbidden pit.

"Which do I want to be?" She closed her eyes. The music cut off halfway through a song. "Both." Kyla held a shot in each hand and downed them swiftly.

"Oh shit, that was dumb!" She started coughing and laughing at the same time. "Dumb, dumb, dumb! That was so dumb!" She did three laps around their table.

Clint laughed along with her. "Are you okay? Yeah, that was really stupid."

"Oh no, I drank yours too!"

"It's okay, it's okay. That was worth it."

The lights to the bar turned on, and they both shielded their eyes. Kyla finally recovered and shook her head. "I can't drive yet." She reached for her phone. "Let me text Chad."

Though he could have, Clint didn't stop her. The darkness of a parked car was nowhere to test how much he truly loved MaryAnn. The bartender who'd been so friendly before now shot them a fatigued look. "We'll figure something out," Clint said.

Outside, the air had cooled, but there was still life on the streets. A food truck, a car with loud bass, and a group of drunk college girls extended down the block. Kyla was frantically texting. "Okay, he said he's too drunk to come get me, but I have to stay at his place if I want to get my car back in the morning." She looked up and smiled, then went back to typing. "Which I need to do because I have so much shit going on and can't wait all day."

Yet another trap, but Clint knew he'd made it too far to collapse now. He bit his lower lip and turned away for a moment as if there was a studio audience to influence his decision.

"I can take you to his place." Clint pulled out his keys and twirled them once. Kyla didn't look at him but instead strode to where their cars were parked.

"Do you think it's safe?" she asked.

"Yeah, what's he gonna do? Run out and punch me?"

She turned her head and connected her hands behind her back, posing. "I meant leaving my car here."

"Nope, it'll probably be gone by sunrise."

Kyla punched him in the shoulder before he unlocked the doors.

Clint stayed focused on the road, but his company affected him more than the alcohol. Instead of giving him an address for her phone, Kyla told him where to turn.

"I think I'm still sober," she said. "I could've driven. Oops, no, there it is."

Clint was content to let her play on her phone. It would all be over soon enough. MaryAnn would never know, and there would be nothing to lie about. He remembered the last time they had sex. It was the morning before he left. One for the road she called it. No, he couldn't hurt her.

"Okay, it's this next stop sign, turn right." Another half block and they were parked on the street in front of a small duplex. "He still lives in campus housing for grad school."

"Hey, you don't need to defend Chad to me," Clint said. "I mean, he didn't leave a light on for you, but still …"

Kyla exhaled. "That boy better be here."

"Do you have a key?"

"No, but I'm expecting one very soon. I have my ways, you know."

No one knew her ways better than Clint.

Kyla got out of the car while he unbuckled his seatbelt but waited back. He didn't need to escort her up the narrow sidewalk and potentially get into some "bro" encounter. As she walked toward the door, he wondered if this was the end of them. Without a goodbye. Potentially, it was the last time he would ever see her. He felt sorry for her in a relationship with a guy who couldn't be troubled to leave a light on out front.

"I don't think he's here," she said after tugging on the door. She knocked three times and then slapped the door with an open hand. A light on the other side of the duplex turned on. Kyla extended her arms.

Clint walked up to the porch, enemy territory. Weird thoughts crossed his mind about the series of events in life that would lead him to the apartment of a guy named Chad who only shared one thing in common with him. Hypotheticals echoed through his head. If he'd never met MaryAnn. If Chad had a gun. A spectrum of possibilities attacked his imagination. He had to shut them up. "Is there a hidden key?"

Kyla looked around. Two empty flower pots and an ashtray were nearby. Clint checked all three but no luck.

"There's a back door," she said. "Worth a shot."

The space between houses was narrow and dark. Crickets chirped nearby. "Gross, I just stepped in a puddle or something. Help."

Clint extended his hand, and she took it. She locked her fingers to his, and Clint found himself turned on. When they got to the backyard, the neighboring house shed some light on them, and she released his hand. "One of them is always back here smoking," Kyla said.

Sure enough, the backdoor was unlocked. She held it open for Clint, who hesitated before entering. "Anyone home?" she called out. "Hello?"

Again, Clint's heart raced, but for a different reason. He imagined a light turning on and a buff dude in boxer shorts who wasn't big on listening, holding a Louisville Slugger. He'd get his ass kicked by a guy named Chad.

"Let me text him again. Follow me." They were in the kitchen, but she led Clint to the front of the house where it was still hard to see anything.

"I should probably get out of here," Clint said.

"Oh, don't worry. He's not the jealous type. He loves comics too, so . . . hold on." Kyla sat on the couch. "He'll probably want to come see your show."

A deeper fear surfaced within Clint: seeing Kyla and Chad together. She'd slipped away from him to someone less worthy. He couldn't perform to an audience knowing his act was the foreplay to Chad and Kyla's date.

Kyla's phone illuminated the room enough for Clint to get his bearings. "Get this," she said. "The bartender can't find Chad's debit card, so . . . yeah, that's where he is."

Clint sat on the couch next to her. His eyes adjusted even after her phone's screen shut off. He grasped for his feelings toward MaryAnn to form a barrier.

"You make this hard," said Kyla.

Don't do anything, Clint told himself. "Why's that?"

"I really like this guy. I think I'm in love, honestly." Her words were razors.

He listened to her breathe, the same innocent, short breaths she would take in her sleep while he lay awake caressing her beneath the sheet on those yesteryear mornings. They should have made something work long distance. His feelings for her were beyond sex. There was an animalistic attraction, but also a chemistry from conversations that inevitably ended in laughter. No other person made him laugh the way she did.

"Kyla, can you promise me something?"

"You never say my name," she cracked a smile. "Must be serious."

"It is," he said. "Promise me you won't tolerate any shit from this guy. I mean anything."

She pressed her head against the spot on his chest where his heart raced. "Aw, you're so sweet." She followed this with an arm into a semi-embrace.

Clint admitted to himself that he hadn't suggested turning on a light either, but still rationalized the situation. This was about caring for a person's well-being. A sentimental attachment was not a sin. And Chad would be there any moment to disrupt the powerful urge of infidelity.

He fought again to think about MaryAnn and if she was the one. If she wasn't, then none of this mattered. But the imminent thought of handing Kyla off to Chad troubled him more. It was inconceivable that she would put her loyalty towards someone else and forget about their annual tradition together.

Kyla pulled her head away, seemingly disinterested now. She yawned and gave a tired sigh. "He's never this late," she whispered. "You can go if you—"

Clint grabbed her face with both hands and kissed her. Then they were on the floor. She rolled over and pulled him with her into the next room. With nothing under her skirt, they finished in moments on the edge of Chad's bed. She lay back, her arms above her head as they exchanged a look. Her eyes were full of surprise, while he delivered a stern expression of, "And don't you ever forget it." Clint slowed his breathing. Any guilt was dwarfed by satisfaction, proving to Kyla that she was still indeed his. Not Chad's. He did not regret the act, only that it wasn't savored.

As he buckled his belt, a car's headlights parked out front. Kyla cursed under her breath but straightened herself to portray the "nothing happened" illusion. "It's okay," she said. "He won't know."

Victorious and confident, Clint left through the front door. Chad was still in his pickup, a spot down from Clint.

"Who are you?" a voice said.

"A friend of Kyla's. Just dropping her off here." He didn't want to make eye contact but needed to ensure there was no threat.

"What? Why are you here?" Chad's voice contained no anger.

"She needed a lift. Nothing happened, dude. You can relax."

"What do I care? We ended that months ago."

TOP SHELF

Charles spotted the unicorn on the top shelf. Devil's Rare, sitting amongst a plethora of rich-brown bottles. It wasn't even priced, but he'd pay whatever they wanted for it.

If he could just reach that high.

His first attempt strained his oblique with a sharp pain as if someone with a spear guarded the bottle. He glanced at the front counter. A line of three kept the shop's lone employee occupied. If a taller patron approached, would Charles be able to lay claim to it even though he technically couldn't remove it from the shelf himself? Just then, two younger gentlemen in suits with loosened ties joined him in the aisle.

"Should we get him something he's never heard of or one of his favorites?" the first man said.

"Who knows? Just pick something." They paused near Charles and scanned the array of bourbons.

Charles took his focus off the prized bottle that these taller men could have easily reached. Would they even know the rarity of the prize above them?

"There's scotch on the next aisle," the second man said. "Wait—look at this. Devil's Rare?"

Charles opened his mouth, but unless the bourbon flowed through his veins, he was unable to stand up for himself.

The second man easily reached the bottle and spun it around in his hands like a football. "Watch it be like two hundred bucks or something," he said. "Barry ain't worth that much." He replaced the treasure to its balcony.

Two hundred bucks? It was worth a grand on the secondary market. These charlatans! "Can't go wrong with Jack Daniels Single Barrel," Charles heard himself say.

Both men gave Charles a look as if he'd suggested a white zinfandel. "Scotch it is," the first one said before leaving the aisle with his pal.

Charles stretched again to reach the bottle. Maybe his courageous interaction added a couple of inches to his stature. Ouch! Again, the oblique.

"You need some help with that?" a woman said. Charles faced her. She was beautiful and maybe a few years his senior. And of course, taller. Much taller.

Charles grimaced. "No, I just . . ."

She stepped closer. "Oh, that's Devil's Rare. I've never seen it in the wild before." Effortlessly, she pulled it down.

Why was everyone snagging his bottle? His temperature rose. He'd never get this chance again. "Actually, I was thinking about purchasing it," Charles said.

"Finders keepers." The woman laughed, but he didn't think it was funny.

Charles adjusted his stance and pushed his lips together. How many times had his height worked against him over the years? There was a friend's wedding when he served as a groomsman only to be paired with the tallest bridesmaid. Or the jokes when waiting in line at the amusement park.

"Sure you don't want it?" She extended the bottle, wiggling it at him like he was a dog and it was a squeaky toy.

Of course he wanted it, but was it worth the cost of his pride? What if she yanked it back? The humiliation on top of missing his chance was too much.

"You know what?" he began. "I dealt with enough bullying in school, but I don't expect it from someone of your age. You think just because you're taller, you're somehow superior. So yeah, go ahead and believe that and take the damn bottle. Small fries like me aren't real people in your eyes."

The woman gulped. "Geez, sensitive? I was going to give you the bottle, but not after that rant."

"Is everything okay, Honey?" The woman's partner appeared. He was at least two inches shorter than Charles.

She leaned over and kissed the top of her mate's head while glaring. The two then walked away with the bottle and Charles' pride.

THE TURN

Dad clicks on the lights and lifts his son from the bed with uncontained enthusiasm.

"This one? How about this one?" A cereal is finally chosen and then it's time to get dressed. "Tie your shoes. Here, let me help." Reluctantly, the son allows it even though he's sure he can do it himself.

Dad loads both sets of golf clubs into the trunk—his shoulders in their prime and the bags so different in size. The son joins him in the front seat having graduated from the contraption of buckles in the back Mom always insists he still use.

They find a nearly empty course on a weekday morning, neither having work nor school. Dad smiles at the group behind them on the fourth tee. "Play through, please." He gives the fellas a wink. "One of us doesn't hit it quite as far."

On and on they play, each hole an orbit around the sun while the shadows shift as subtly as their change in height. Everything is even at the turn. The day's heat fades and dries the greens and putts roll too fast. Dad's sweat traces each wrinkle on his forehead. His son's skin tans against growing muscle. The trees along the fairway are much taller than before.

The lake at sixteen is always a problem for Dad's shorter drives, and the son cringes as Dad grabs his back after his follow-through. *Plunk!* "That's okay, hit another," the son says before noticing a threesome who has caught up with them.

Dad rubs his back some more. "Gentlemen, go ahead," the son says before joining Dad on the bench.

As they replace the flag on the final hole, the sun lowers its angle against the gray on Dad's head. "Burgers and beers are on me," the son says. He guides Dad through the menu. "Which sides do you want? You get two."

The son unloads both bags from the trunk as Dad hobbles to the door. "Let me help you with your shoes. Have a seat on the porch swing." Dad rolls his eyes because if it wasn't for a tight back he'd do it himself.

The son helps his dad into bed, tired grunts are exchanged. "Good night." The son clicks off Dad's bedroom light.

THE ONE WITH SEX IN IT

Chris gazed at Amanda so often he almost didn't care if she knew. It had been easier to view her while the sun was still setting and the cheap sunglasses he borrowed from his brother shielded his focused gaze. For most of the afternoon, he sat silent, facing the lake, but straining his eyes sideways to look at the nearby female perfection barely contained in a bright pink bikini. He played possum for hours as his brother and the rest of the upperclassmen emptied beer after beer, tossing them into a makeshift pit in the shore's coarse sand.

Lake Massy had no waves other than small ripples when everyone splashed around. The private property belonged to a parent whose son was currently backflipping off the tiny floating dock where the water grew deeper. For hours, someone always seemed to be laughing.

Now that the sun was down, Chris could relax his diligent use of sunscreen. His older brother Austin had been blessed with a darker skin tone and brown hair, while Chris carried on the redheaded trademark from his mother's side of the family. It was all his mother left him. The pale skin and freckles led to his nickname Gin, short for Ginger. None of his friends called him Gin. He was still Chris to them. Or Austin's younger brother. But some of Austin's buddies deemed him Ginger the first time he was around. The girls said it was mean, so they trimmed it down to Gin, a tolerable compromise.

Maybe it was pity that first inspired Amanda to saunter over and acknowledge him. "Do you ever get in the water?"

This was permission for eye contact. "I might. I don't want to get the truck all wet when we leave."

She shrugged and entered the water with a tipsy walk as he watched. His father's Ram was the only reason Chris was there. Austin didn't teach his little brother much. They didn't play catch. There were no chats about how to land girls like Amanda. However, during the week their father was away, Austin trained his fourteen-year-old brother to become Fairview's number one designated driver for the upperclassmen.

"You can save someone's life or you can stay home by yourself," Austin always phrased it. Chris didn't argue. He was more than happy to observe the shenanigans of the cool kids, especially with Amanda present. Content to be a fly on the wall, he became a party asset by driving as many as two dozen intoxicated hellions home. They would often pile into the cab of the Dodge, texting their addresses to the boy behind the wheel who calmly dropped each of them off to no gratuity other than "Thanks Gin!" or "You my Gin-ga!"

106

Twilight raced towards darkness during the new moon, so he could barely see the group collected on the dock. Amanda's silhouette was a work of art. Only the sound of laughter and a cooler opening and shutting filled the void for some time. The group's volume would swell and then return to almost a whisper over and over. Chris checked his phone. Dead. Mosquitoes aggravated his skin, and the temperature never relented even in darkness.

Another crescendo in the conversation led to a chorus of "Aww" like someone had just produced a puppy. "Gin, get out here!" Austin called.

"I'm good," he said.

"We're playing a game. You have to play too." The voice might have been Amanda's.

Chris stood and kicked off his flip-flops. The ground was cooler, but the water was still bath-like. "I can barely see," he said. The floating dock was a short swim away to where the water was just deep enough that no one could stand with their head above it except for Tommy, Fairview High's starting center.

"Join us," someone said as he got nearer to the dock. A hand pulled him up and he found himself seated along the perimeter facing inward like everyone else. It felt even darker now. His brother was on the other side of the chain of bare knees, laughing about something as one of the Bonner twins began explaining from the middle of the circle. "You gotta sit guy girl guy girl." Chris couldn't remember if it was Abby or Grace. They weren't identical, but he never interacted with either enough to distinguish which was which.

"The person to your right is the one who matters," she continued. Chris looked to his right. "I'm Grace," she said. "Or am I lying?"

"Shut up, Abby," the twin said. "No messing with Gin."

Chris's heart swelled a bit at Grace's defense. So Abby was on his right. She was the more mischievous of the two. She stopped cheerleading after her sophomore year while her sister continued to wow the gym with handsprings and backflips during timeouts. Abby's claim to fame was a one-minute keg stand in her prom dress on a spring night three months ago when Chris's DD-ing was starting to grow in popularity. Abby and her drunken escapades had the safety net of Chris always getting her and others home safely.

Grace looked at Chris. "You're gonna need a beer for this."

"He doesn't drink," Austin said. "Or else how is anyone getting home?"

"No one's going home tonight," somebody said. Others agreed. "Get on with the rules."

"You have to guess if the person on your right is still a virgin, and if you think they aren't, you have to guess the age they lost it at."

"Oh, we already played this at Tommy's house that one time," one of the girls said.

"No fair, Taylor gets off too easy," Austin said.

Taylor leaned into Chris's left shoulder. "Maybe your big brother doesn't know everything." She laughed and then bit Chris's shoulder. "Rarrr!"

Thankfully, the darkness hid his blush.

"Now here's the fun part. Once you're wrong, you have to get in the water. Or, if the person next to you gets it right, you have to get in . . . but your suit stays on the dock."

A group roar. "Looks like it'll be a full moon after all tonight!" Tommy said.

"Hope the leeches went to sleep."

"I'll start," Austin said. "Don't even bother sitting down, Grace. You were sixteen."

"Thanks, bestie," she said. "Glad you're so good at keeping secrets."

Abby leaned over to Chris. "He went to a different school. Dude was such a tool."

Grace exhaled and jumped into the water, splashing everyone near Austin. Moments later, her top, then bottom, landed in the middle of the circle.

Chris's heart dropped. Were they really doing this? Why did he have to be a part of it? Was he the only virgin? He stared at his brother for help, but Austin took no notice. Minutes later, half the dock had emptied into the lake, and a pile of suits lay scattered in front of Chris.

Finally, it was Taylor's turn. "I'm gonna go out on a limb and say . . . Wait, how old are you, Gin? Fifteen?"

"He's fourteen," Austin said.

"Yikes," Taylor said. "Then you're like my aunt's daiquiris. Vir to the gin. Hey, Gin! Get it?" She laughed to herself. "Gin, get in! Oh, I'm on fire."

Chris looked to his brother again.

Austin only shrugged and said, "You want to hang with the big boys and girls, you have to play too."

There were more people in the water than on the dock now. Chris forced himself to jump in and somehow found the courage to untie his drawstrings. Everyone else was doing it, so what did he have to fear? All their cellphones were safe on the shore, and the water hid everything. Plus, if the girls could do it, what did he have to fear? And thank God the water was still ridiculously warm.

He set his trunks on the edge of the dock where he'd been sitting. The game wouldn't last much longer at this pace.

He swam away from the group towards the shallower water that came up to his shoulders and watched in amazement. One by one, the others leaped into the water and chucked their garments back to the dock. His friends would never partake in stuff like this. Getting drunk and naked around each other? Not on his friend group's horizon.

Suddenly, Amanda was yelling. "You are! I knew it! Austin is still a virgin, I win! I fucking win!" He watched the goddess cannonball off the dock and then reach behind her back to untie her straps. He caught a glimpse of a topless Amanda, and his heart pounded through his chest. Now was a good time to isolate himself from the older kids.

As they all swam about, Chris drifted back to the side of the dock facing the shore, safely alone. There was a support beam where he could plant his feet and keep his head above the water just enough. When no one was looking, he would reach up, grab his trunks, and make his way back to his post at the truck.

"Gin? You still out here?" It was Amanda.

"He probably drowned, no biggie," Austin said.

"All good," Chris yelled.

"Oh, Gi-in," Amanda called. "*Where aaare you?*"

He was no longer alone on his side of the dock. Amanda emerged, treading water, a nymph with her hair slicked back. "There you . . . are." She was breathing hard from swimming.

Chris felt the day's worth of heat radiating off his skin. "Yep, just waiting here for everyone to . . . maybe not be naked."

"You aren't breaking the rules," she drifted towards him, "are you?"

He shook his head no as she swam closer. "Oh, you found a spot to stand." She was now directly in front of him, her arms rapidly sweeping across the water's surface. "Let me see if I can touch." Her head disappeared for a second. "Nope!"

They stared at each other, the group's laughter faint in the distance. "It's okay, Gin," she whispered. "You can look at me as long as you want. A lot of guys do."

She let out a giggle. "What if I just—"

Then she embraced him.

More than she meant to.

Chris gasped. "Oh God, I—" It took only a moment, and then it was over.

Amanda's eyes bulged.

"I'm sorry, I'm sorry!" Chris said as she released him.

"Shh, shh, shh. Jesus, that was—I didn't mean to, I wasn't trying to . . . Oh my God."

Chris couldn't stop shaking his head. He covered his face.

Amanda let out a laugh. "I mean, that doesn't really count. I didn't know you were . . . ready for me. I mean, I see the way you look at me, so maybe I should've known, but yeah, I was just going to let you feel my boobs or something and then wham bam, and, God, you younger guys. I mean, oh God, you're so fucking young. Do you even know what you just did? Of course, you know, but I mean, you didn't mean to, right?"

He shook his head.

"Okay, then that doesn't even count. I mean, you can say it does, but you don't get to tell everyone I took your V-card. Fuck, I turn 18 in two weeks, so yeah, I would have to go to jail if that got out. You can't—"

"I won't."

"You better not 'cause, yeah, that was your fault, not mine. I didn't know you were gonna be like . . . ready." She laughed again. A nervous chuckle.

"Amanda, are you molesting my brother?" Austin called out from the blackness.

The two exchanged a shocked look. "He didn't see, he didn't see," she whispered. She swam back a stroke.

"Just making sure he's okay," she called back. "You jealous?"

She turned back to Chris and smiled. "He is, isn't he?"

Chris shrugged. "Can I put my suit back on?"

"You probably should. Way too many naked girls swimming around." She took a few backstrokes, exposing her entire chest before returning to a steady tread. "I'm glad I was your first time, even if . . ." She turned and swam away quickly, her bare back disappearing into the darkness.

Part 6

"You can say what you want
but don't act like you care
It takes more than one person
to decide what's fair"

"Spitting Venom"
by Modest Mouse

We're not always proud of our actions, right? These stories illustrate that starting with "Extra Butter." "Whatever Works" has the collection's only married couple. "A Ride Home" probably happened to me in some form, while "Positive/Negative" was written for a graduate school assignment from a few years back.

EXTRA BUTTER

Emma was two spots behind Kevin in line. She could have ordered for him. "Large popcorn, large Sprite."

Their running joke replayed in her head:

"Do you want anything?"

"None for me, but get extra butter."

She'd help him empty the bucket before the end of the opening credits. And the Sprite? She did her best to leave just enough so that the sputtering sound of the shared straw would be during his turn, not hers.

Now, without her, he'd bloat himself trying to finish it all alone. She knew this for a fact. He admitted that during these Sunday matinees he attended solo, he could never finish the bucket.

And without her, surely his heart was a gaping hole. His decision, not hers, three weeks prior. She shouldn't have asked where he saw it going. Instead of pulling her into his arms and handing her a key to his apartment, he said, "You're right. I don't think I can do this anymore."

"No, that's not what I meant," she said. "Please, please, just listen to me. I like us together."

"I wish I felt the same, but before we get serious . . ."

She watched the pimply kid behind the counter attempt to swipe Kevin's card. Her temperature rose. *Before they got serious?* They spent 13 out of 22 nights together. There were another handful of times he could have stayed over but had to work early in the morning. They'd been to five movies, two minigolf courses, and a play. Did he know the effort it took for her to stay awake for a play?

She would ask him a trick question. Did he enjoy movies by himself more? If he said no, she would suggest joining him. They'd be back together by the second act. If he said yes then she'd bring up the fact that he was a liar because he had told her—no, *promised* her—movies were always better with her by his side. So which was it, Kevin?

His transaction finished and the line moved forward as he turned towards the butter machine. She should've acknowledged him sooner. He couldn't embrace her while carrying his cargo. She focused on his eyes and knew she was smiling too much. She couldn't help it. That's what he did to her.

"Oh, hi," he said.

"Old habits die hard I guess." Yeah, that would work. He didn't own this theater. She smiled back and laughed for some reason. She was about to ask her trap of a question when she noticed the tray he carried. A medium popcorn at best, and then a Sprite and what appeared to be a cola. Both smalls.

Despite the jab to her heart, she would not break. One did not take eight weeks of acting and improv class after college just to stare stunned. "A new partner?" She nodded at his tray.

"Something like that," he said.

"Well, we're claiming theater six today." She laughed again. It was his turn to be surprised. "I better order."

"We're in theater three, so—"

"A large popcorn, a box of Mike & Ike's, a Sprite, and, oh what was it? A root beer." That ought to leave him reeling. She wouldn't turn and let him complete his goodbye until her order was fulfilled. The total would cost her a half-week of groceries, but after this devastation, she couldn't imagine herself ever being hungry again.

The tray was awkward in her hands, and she thought of one more base to cover. "I lost a bet, so it was my turn." That's right Kevin, someone else playful enough to make bets with her. Someone comfortable enough to let his woman not only fetch but pay for the concessions. They were already at that level in their new relationship. Was he squirming at this realization? Good.

"It was nice to see you."

Regret. She could hear it in his voice. Before she could counter with the typical cliché, his "date" approached.

"Uncle Kevin, the movie is starting."

The child looked up at her and then back to him.

"Ours probably is too," she said. "It was nice seeing you."

She watched them walk to the butter machine. Kevin laughed as he pretended to almost drop everything. It was endearing how he let the kid hold the drinks while he pumped in the butter. What a man. He wasn't going to get away. "Uncle Kevin" and his niece finally disappeared towards theater three. Emma turned, dumped her tray into the trash, then exited the theater.

She'd accidentally run into him again at his Thursday night happy hour.

WHATEVER WORKS

The biggest difference in Grant's marriage versus his brother's was how he and Donna kept their arguments private. Eleven years of tiffs, stand-offs, silent battles, and everything in between were all behind them. There'd be more, but he and his wife would handle them with the same efficient communication they'd mastered through life's hardships. So when Ethan and Lisa woke everyone up with a shouting match that not even the morning tide could smother, all Grant could do was fold his arms and laugh.

The sun rose behind clouds, and the sand was cold under his toes. The younger couple lowered their voices in his presence.

"Two weeks, Grant. Two weeks, and she loses it already." Ethan threw his arms up before he began clawing under the remaining chairs that formed a messy circle around the ashes from last night.

"The necklace?" Grant asked.

"I'll find it. It's out here somewhere," Lisa said. "Unless somebody took it inside." She paused her search and looked back up to the beach house where three other couples had yet to appear.

"What's the last thing you remember?" Grant asked. He wasn't sure who would answer.

"Ethan being a jerk, so I took it off and threw it at him."

"How was I being a jerk?" He was yelling again. "I spend half my savings on—"

"Like that! Always throwing it in my face."

"Yes, I remember that part," Grant said. "I'm quite sure you made your point while the rest of us headed to bed." He reached down and collected three mostly empty beer cans and let their contents drip out into the sand.

"You slept in your Escalade?" Ethan asked.

Grant nodded with a misplaced sense of triumph.

"Did Donna?" Lisa asked.

"Nope. She had her headphones." Grant folded his arms again proudly. "Sometimes we do," he popped up on his toes, "whatever works."

Lisa returned her attention to her husband. "So when I threw it at you, did you catch it?"

"I thought I did. Hell, I don't know. I was so . . . God, how much did we drink?"

"You were sitting with your back to the house," Grant said. "I thought the necklace was with you. Maybe in your lap for a while when Lisa . . ."

"When I told you I hated you and went to bed," Lisa said.

The three of them each let out a mild laugh, forgetting how valuable the jewelry was for a moment. Lisa walked toward the water while Ethan stood by his brother.

"That puts it on you, doesn't it?" Grant said. "I remember her throwing it at you, I think."

"I don't," said Ethan. "Would Donna know?"

"Ha, no. She was the first one out. I tucked her in and then slept in the backseat. Pretty comfortable too. Not a bed, but . . ."

"Sorry," Ethan said. He brought his hand to his chin and dragged his toes through the sand.

"You sleep in the same room last night?" Grant asked.

"Maybe? Wait . . . yeah. I did." His face lit back up. "In fact, yeah, we did a lot more than sleep, and that's when I put the necklace back on her. I know it! It was our best sex in months."

"So then it's inside," Grant said. "Why isn't it still on her neck? Are you sure?"

"I distinctly remember putting it on her neck."

"You're sure?"

"It was the only thing she was wearing," Ethan said behind his hand before calling to his wife. "Hey Lisa, babe, it's not out here. It's gotta be inside with your stuff somewhere."

The three of them trudged toward the beach house. It seemed to be waking up as they climbed the stairs to the back deck where Donna had her head down on the table next to an untouched cup of coffee. Grant leaned over and kissed her on the temple. She sat up, still half-asleep, her headache almost visible.

Ethan saw it first. Then Lisa. Finally Grant.

"How did I end up wearing this?" Donna said, grasping the necklace.

A RIDE HOME

When Grace took off her gloves I couldn't help myself. I reached and held her hand. The darkness made it easier. Or maybe it was the four drinks. She looked away, surprised, but with a smile. She didn't pull away.

From behind the wheel, Richard kept babbling about how great the party was compared to other work gatherings. None of us had expected our boss to push that many drinks on us.

I hoped Grace's head wasn't spinning like mine. Our contact steadied me, and I thought I felt a slight squeeze as we came to the light. I rubbed the top of her hand with my thumb. She looked down at our little secret, and again a tiny smile appeared. Our backseat pact of infatuation unfolded while an oblivious Richard ranted about Kevin McDonald's cubicle decorations and what we'd do the rest of the night.

Richard glanced back at us in the mirror. "Should we go to Harry's Pub next?"

God no, not Harry's.

"Okay," Grace said.

"Good with me. I love that place," I said.

Grace looked out her window, silent again. Fine then. We'll hold hands at Harry's too.

Richard changed the station three times before finally settling on Seger.

Content with her hand in mine, we rode to Harry's and parallel parked across the street. I got out and hurried around to the other side and opened Grace's door. Richard could find out now. He could tell the whole office. They'd get used to it.

Richard leaned back. "On second thought, I'm not feeling it. Can you Uber home?"

"Sure," I said. Then I reached for Grace's hand.

"I think I'm just going to have him drive me home now," she said. It was the first time she looked me in the eye the whole night.

I don't remember which of us closed the door, nor did I look both ways before crossing the street. What did I care if a bus hit me? As I got to the pub's entrance and looked back, Grace was getting into the front seat with a much larger smile.

Unfortunately, the office would certainly hear about this too.

POSITIVE/NEGATIVE

Cody walked by the pregnancy tests three times. On his first lap, he made eye contact with a sizable woman reaching for a box of tampons. The second trip yielded a flustered mother of four, two of them screaming. But on his third pass, he balked on his own. Was it really necessary? Why did he always assume the worst?

Jilly was different, and at four months into the relationship, he wanted to feel optimistic for once. At least more than the mini-relationships he'd plagued himself with in his early twenties. He wasn't just going to ask her, "Are you pregnant?" Women are supposed to tell you those things, and maybe he didn't know her as well as he thought he did. What else was she keeping from him?

Cody frowned at the pricing. $4.99 for a one-pack, but only $6.99 for a 3-pack. Normally, he'd choose the obvious value, but there was no chance of giving her a second test. One would answer everything. So despite his frugal instincts, he picked up the single. It rattled a bit in his hand as he walked past the rows of condoms. He smirked under the aisle sign that read "Family Planning" as if some happy married couple would stroll through these products with a checklist and a calendar.

He walked out of the pharmacy aisle, wishing he'd used a cart. The box made him blush and his temperature rose. Just two weeks ago, he'd purchased a dozen red roses from this same store. People acknowledged him then, but with smiles. The flowers had made Jilly cry.

"It's the first time a guy has ever . . ." He'd never made a girlfriend cry before, but he had a feeling she was experiencing more than just flowers. She didn't just weep; she bawled. Uncontrollably. And that was his first clue that something was off about her.

"How did I get so lucky? You deserve better than me." The words came out during half a box of tissues. And then the question all his former girlfriends asked at some point: "How have you never been in a long-term relationship before? I don't believe you."

Admitting his fertility issues always ended it. Not right away, but each former girlfriend found a way to make things fizzle.

The self-checkout lane had a line extending into an aisle. Hello again, mother of four. Who cares, Cody thought as he stood behind the lone customer at a regular register. The cashier had probably seen worse purchases than a pregnancy test.

When it was his turn, the cashier needed two swipes over the scanner. She was older and skinny with outdated bangs. "How's your evening going?" she asked.

"I'll let you know in the next hour," he said.

"What?"

Cody gestured at the box. "Results pending." He let out a little laugh as she dropped the box into a bag.

She didn't seem to grasp the magnitude of his purchase. How could someone be so dense? After he paid, she tore off his receipt and told him to have a nice night. He let the encounter distract him on the way home. What joke could he have made? How could a person not comprehend what he'd just remarked?

Either way, the first step was over. The next challenge was getting Jilly to take the test without her knowing. She wasn't quite as oblivious.

They didn't normally drink on Wednesdays, but he craved a mild beer buzz to survive the upcoming task. Jilly arrived straight from her job and kissed him like she normally did before sitting on the couch for *Jeopardy*. He noticed her purse was still over her shoulder.

"Planning on staying?" he asked with a nod at her arm.

"Oh, sorry," she said. "I'm trying to stay off my phone tonight, so I'm keeping it in here." She patted the Guess emblem and let the strap off her arm.

Maybe she had already run some tests on herself. Was there some secret that dwarfed pregnancy? Maybe she only had two months to live. Jilly never went more than a few minutes without checking her phone. He was right that something was up.

Cody went for a beer to the fridge in the adjacent kitchen. The show's theme song music played from the living room. They'd missed the opening segment. "Do you love me?" he asked while searching for a bottle opener in a drawer.

"What?"

He knew she heard him, but it was easier to ask from there. "Do you want a beer?"

"No, Sweetie. And that's not what you said the first time."

He sat on the couch, angling himself towards her. "So you heard me?"

"Why are you drinking tonight? Oh God, what's wrong?"

He stared at the television. "What is mitosis?" Cody said. One of the contestants echoed his correct response. She turned back to the television, and neither could answer the next few clues. "I asked if you loved me."

"What is *insecure*?" Jilly said. "You know I love you. I know I love you."

"How?"

"I just do, okay?" She looked hurt.

He was pressing too soon.

She folded her arms in a dramatic pout. "Well, how did you know when you loved me?"

He adjusted his legs. "One morning after you spent the night, I made toast."

Jilly laughed. "Seriously, you think you can explain it because you made me toast that one time?"

"You remember?"

"I do. It hasn't happened since."

"We usually stay at your place."

"Fair enough."

"My toaster is old, and when the two slices popped out, one was perfect and one was burnt." He sipped his beer. "And without thinking, I took the burnt piece and gave you the perfect one."

Jilly wilted on the couch. The waterworks were released again, much to his satisfaction. Overly emotional, just like the article said. "I think I'm out of tissues. I have paper towels." He scrambled back to the kitchen and tore two sheets off. "Sorry they're not as soft." He let her cry while he scored a few more correct answers before the round ended.

"I don't deserve you." She'd said it often lately.

"Why do you think that?"

"You're just too good for me. I can't believe . . ."

"Okay, stop it. I'm not fishing here," he said. "Double

Jeopardy is starting."

Jilly blew her nose as Cody scoffed at the new categories. How did anyone know anything about opera?

At the end of the round, Jilly finally got up to use his bathroom. He tensed and waited. What if she figured out what he was up to?

"Cody."

He walked down the small hallway towards the closed door. She yelled again. "Cody!"

"I'm right here."

She cracked the door. "Your toilet is broken. I'm pulling the handle, and it isn't flushing."

"I'll fix it." He tried to sound labored.

"I don't want you to see my pee." Thank God that was all. Jilly laughed, reluctant to let him pass.

"Just put the lid down. I can fix the tank."

She looked back, and he could tell she was debating whether to attempt it herself. Did he need to remind her of the time she got a new television and couldn't attach the cable box? Or the time her refrigerator froze everything solid because she turned the settings the wrong way?

"You answer Final Jeopardy, and I'll fix the toilet."

She let out a disgusted sigh but returned to the living room.

Should he close the door? He'd already opened the pregnancy test box and placed it safely under the sink beneath a spare tube of Colgate. He stuck his head back out into the hallway.

Jilly had remained standing. "What?" she said. "Are you grossed out?"

He faked a laugh. "Relax," he said. "Let a man do his job." He closed the door and locked it. He opened the tank's lid and reattached the chain to the handle. Earlier, he'd drained as much water as he could out of the bowl to

128

avoid diluting his sample. Just before he carried out this despicable deed, he caught himself in the mirror. Maybe this is why he had so much trouble with women. He didn't deserve to reproduce.

And then he dipped the stick.

The next issue was the five-minute waiting period for the result. She'd grow suspicious if he was in there too long.

"Cody?" She was just outside the door.

He flushed the toilet. "Almost finished." He placed the stick on a wad of toilet paper, thick enough to wrap a hypothetical child in, and stuck it back under the sink.

He looked at his face again in the mirror. He was shaking. "Just gotta wash my hands," he called out.

"Did you fix it?"

He opened the door. "I think so. I'll check next time I have to go."

His face was giving him away. He hurried back to the living room. "We missed Final Jeopardy, didn't we?" Uh-oh. His voice was shaky too. He reached for his beer and guzzled half the bottle.

"Sorry if that disgusted you, but maybe you should live in a better apartment."

He sipped more, staying silent. She could hang herself. He already sensed the result of the test.

"Oh God, I wasn't asking you to move in with me. I know you've never . . ."

"I'm not ready for that either," he said.

She shot him a look suggesting his tone insulted her. "How do I know you've never been with anyone as long as me? I mean, you always tell me that, but I still don't believe it."

He loved her. He really did. But he knew he wasn't the one for her. To be fair, he didn't have any solid proof of cheating to back his suspicions. No late-night texts. No lame excuses for why she was late. His theory was only based on her emotions whenever he did something sweet for her. Only guilt and a trimester could make a person weep the way she did.

"Unless you would want to live with me? Maybe someday?" She was almost whispering. Did she know she was pregnant too? He really should have picked up more tissues.

He stared back at her. If there was as much guilt as he thought, it would break her on its own. "When was it?" he asked.

"When was what?"

He could see the question reverberating through her mind until she realized that he knew. Her brief silence told him he was right.

"And you're pregnant." His words were as casual as someone commenting on a painting.

"What?" Her face twisted from amused to shocked to confused. "You think we're having a baby?" Just like on Jeopardy, the question sounded more like a statement.

"No," he said, looking down at his feet. From all the planning to get him this far, he'd failed to prepare his words.

"Okay, so you're asking if I'm late? Is that what you were asking? Because I'd rather not—"

"When did you cheat on me?"

This time her face radiated instant anger. "Okay, what the hell is going on? I'm pregnant, and I cheated on you, huh?"

He tipped his head to the side.

"And if I am pregnant? You assume you didn't do it? You're not exactly the most careful guy you know." She reached for the paper towels.

Despite the outcome, a small part of his heart still hurt

for her. He did love her before this.

She blew her nose. "I'm not sure if I'm pregnant, okay? I haven't tested myself yet. What are you, some psychic or something?"

He prayed she wouldn't realize his scheme. "It's okay. You are. And I know it's not mine."

Her face soaked in tears, she threw her hands out to her sides.

Cody tried to counter her with a calm demeanor. He sat down at his previous spot. "You know how you're always surprised that I've never been with anyone for very long?"

She folded her arms and nodded.

"It's because I'm sterile. My doctor said I can't have kids. Your baby belongs to whoever you cheated with."

She stood up and snatched her purse from the couch. The crinkled paper towel mass fell to the floor. She didn't turn to look at him again but spat out a stern goodbye before slamming the door.

I should have done that differently, Cody thought. He picked up the paper towels, unable to believe how soaked they were. Then he chugged the rest of his beer before the inevitable trip back to the bathroom.

Later that night, Cody found himself at the same cashier, buying a six-pack of a local lager he'd been meaning to try.

He was surprised when she addressed him. "Well? What'd it say?"

"Negative."

Part 7

"These walls are
paper thin and
everyone hears every
little sound,
Everyone's a
voyeurist,
they're watching me
watch them watch me
right now"

Paper Thin Walls
by Modest Mouse

At first, I thought this next story didn't belong in the book. It began as just part one, but after I shared it online, someone suggested I keep going. Its earlier drafts were goofy at best. I shared it with my students, and they encouraged me to revise it until I was satisfied, so I did. And yes, the title quotes that Offspring song.

As for the final story, I kept hearing "Mary Jane's Last Dance" by Tom Petty randomly on the radio. It must've been a half-dozen times in one week. I thought about how the lyrics painted the picture of a town and then I took some liberties in writing it (making sure I wasn't too on the nose). It's the longest piece in the book, but I hope you find it worth the wait.

THE MORE YOU SUFFER

Part 1

Michael's phone vibrated on the cafe table. She was near. Within fifty or so feet, according to the settings on the dating app. When she entered, he realized his heart didn't need the third cup of coffee.

He watched her order and wondered if the thin, white sweater over the black leggings was a new outfit for the occasion. For him. There was no one ahead or behind her, so the view was his alone. Her hair was different, unlike any of the pictures. A little shorter now, and browner. The summer's streaks of gold had faded.

Michael had thumbed through all five of her profile photos so many times. A 5K race in black shorts and a pink tank top. Cropped from the rest of the group, a bridesmaid in a baby blue gown. Hiking in a brown jacket with some guy (probably her brother, but it was still his least favorite). Wrigley Field in a pin-striped Cubs jersey with her grandpa. And then there was his favorite, the picture that framed her face. It must have been hours he'd stared at her smile above the two yellow straps on otherwise bare shoulders—a body of water in the background almost as blue as her eyes. Her skin was tan except for a pale outline from wearing sunglasses. Someday he would be in a picture next to her.

He pulled the bill of his hat down a bit and then waved to get her attention. She flashed a surprised smile and walked over. "Sorry I'm late. You wouldn't think a library would be so busy."

As she steadied her mug, he steadied his voice.

"Hello, I'm Tim. Of course."

"Sarah," she said. "Nice to meet you."

He exhaled relief as she sat down. *Don't screw it up this time.* He looked into her eyes, as blue as before. "Pretty good coffee here, right?"

She sipped and flinched. "Oh, still hot. Guess I'll never learn." She set her cup down and studied him.

He held his breath and returned her gaze. It was so amazing to see her in person. "So what are—"

"Tim, you remind me of someone." She leaned back.

"That's weird. I just moved to Chicago, so maybe—"

"No. Oh my god, no. It's you! Again?"

"Wait, just listen."

"No! What is this, the third time? You're Brian . . . or Alex. I remember you." She stood up, almost knocking the chair over. "You can't keep doing this."

The barista was probably staring at him.

"Just let me explain," he said, but he knew he couldn't. "If you got to know me, you'd see we have so much . . ." She was gone.

Michael opened the app on his phone.

Edit profile. Name: James.

He pocketed his phone. Perhaps a more direct method was necessary. Time to visit some libraries.

Part 2

Bookshelves made it easy to stay unnoticed. Stealth mode was fun. To Michael, it wasn't hiding, but rather letting Sarah avoid any distractions on the job. He wouldn't dare come between her and the books she placed back on the shelves of the second floor, though he made a game of touching them shortly after she had. There was one close call last week, but a pull on his hood and a pivot behind the biographies was all it took.

Certain shifts held a challenge to locate her, which gave him a stir of pleasure like an addict finally receiving his dose. Today he couldn't imagine what duty would keep a librarian assistant from the floor for so long. Was there an office or special room where she organized stacks? She would be isolated and lonely, left to reflect on her senseless rejection of him. How difficult would it be to find this chamber? He'd need either a keycard or an ajar door. Then she'd listen to him. She'd have to. He'd stay as calm as when she left her coffee behind for him to happily finish. His mouth on the edge where her lipstick had stained. His lips where hers had just been. A time-elapsed kiss.

By the time the afternoon light faded from the windows, he surmised she wasn't there. He hoped she wasn't ill. It wasn't like her to take a Thursday off. Concerned, he approached the old woman at the information desk. "Excuse me, I'm looking for someone who suggested a book to me last week. Her name was . . . I don't remember. Young, very pretty."

"Sarah?" The woman raised her glasses to her forehead and smiled. "I'm afraid she's no longer on our team here."

He stared at her face, evaluating his chances for more information. "Oh. She was very friendly. I don't suppose you can tell me—" He shook his head to dismiss the suggestion before the woman could. "What contemporary poetry books would you recommend, ma'am . . .?"

He could call her Helen, she said, and after admitting her ignorance of the genre, she led him to a few titles after a bit of research. She escorted him downstairs to the self-checkout counter before pausing and offering one last bit of advice. "You should visit our newly remodeled Lozano branch. You might even run into a familiar face there."

"Oh, it's reopened? I can't thank you enough," he said. The woman had saved him days of searching. "That might be a little closer to my apartment anyway."

"Such a charming smile on you," the woman said. "Are you always this happy?"

Minutes later, though nearing closing time, he circled through the freshly painted parking garage of a different library. He let his car coast over to the book deposit where he returned both choices the old woman had suggested. Daylight would be scarce on the way home, but a pale, white glow from the garage lights allowed him to cruise each of the three floors until he found his target on the middle level: a red hatchback with a scuffed rear bumper.

This would do. He parked behind a pole, hungry for what was sure to be a perfect view.

Part 3

Michael squeezed the steering wheel so hard his knuckles cracked. Who was the man in the suit? He was not her perfect match! Why was she laughing so much? This man had the nerve to block his view! He had earned this little glimpse of perfection and now a tall, slender man was standing between them.

He finally exhaled as the man let her leave without more than a pat on the shoulder. For Sarah's own good, he would follow the man to make sure he wasn't some psycho.

It wasn't a bar he'd visited before, fairly busy for a

Thursday. He waited until the intrusive stranger was halfway through his first drink before sitting next to him.

"Either you're overdressed or I'm underdressed," Michael opened with. "I guess the ladies will have to decide." His laugh wasn't echoed.

"I'm sorry, are you joking?" the man asked.

"James, joking of course." Whatever worked.

"Donald Benson. Well, just Don, I'm off the clock." They shook hands. "And I've got bad news for you if you're waiting for a woman to decide." This time, only Don laughed.

Michael looked around. By the looks of the decor and the clientele, there wouldn't be any women there . . . ever. Don was never a threat to steal his Sarah! This relief shadowed any discomfort he felt. "I'm looking for a different job myself," said Michael as Don poked at his phone. Was he texting Sarah? Making sure she got home okay?

"Sorry," Don said. "Work project." He took a sip of beer. His upper lip wore the foam for a brief moment. "Did you say you were looking for work?"

"Yes, but I don't want to impose. You're trying to relax—"

"Sorry." Another text took his attention. "What kind of work are you into?"

Michael hesitated. This question came quicker than he'd planned. "Mostly museums, but anything academic. What kind of business do you work in?"

Don finished his glass and set it down, missing the coaster. "How do you feel about libraries?"

On the entire drive home, Michael cradled the business card in his palm. It wasn't a keycard, but it could lead to one. His options were numerous. He grew giddy as he parked next to his neighbor's truck and slipped the card into his wallet. In the future, he would be able to tell Sarah about these marathon days. She'd laugh like crazy. "You seriously hit on a guy in a gay bar?" It was the only way, he would tell her. "I was determined to get another chance with you."

Michael smiled. The day was a win. Moments later, his phone buzzed. It was Angie. "Where the hell have you been?"

He couldn't wait to replace her.

Part 4

The curved yet not creased business card looked like Michael had possessed it for months. The sweat from his palm had withered it. He didn't need the contact information. Donald's name was enough.

The library answered on the first ring.

"Chicago Public Library, Manning Branch. How may I direct your call?"

"Is Helen available?" The hold music was faint, making him impatient.

"This is Helen, how may I help you?"

"Helen, it's Donald."

"Donald?"

"Benson."

"Oh, Don. My my, aren't we formal this morning?"

He smacked his free palm into his temple and tried to rebound his mistake with a laugh. "Sorry, so many calls today. Hectic."

"You don't sound like yourself."

The less talk, the better. "Turns out we didn't get all of Sarah's information on the transfer. You have her cell?" Michael held his breath.

"Wouldn't HR have that, Don? I don't think I'm allowed to . . ."

He should've waited a few more days. Rehearsed to see if it sounded right. He was already furious. "Helen. Remember how hectic I said things had been?"

"I know but—"

"If I call HR back, they'll want answers for a dozen other loose ends . . ." He was out of words. Lies. So he waited.

"Eight. One. Five . . ."

The animosity was in Helen's voice now, each digit so deliberate. The numbers went straight to his memory, and at this moment, nothing in his brain was more important. He wouldn't need Helen to repeat them. The real Don would be in for quite a cold front the next time he talked to Helen in person!

"That it?"

"Thanks." He sang the numbers before dialing them and hitting send, daring himself to let her answer. That impulse ended with common sense. He added the contact and used the stored screenshot from her dating profile, the lake one, of course. The things he'd do to stand next to her in that picture.

Michael tried to collect himself as he began a text message. "Hi Sarah, it's Don Benson. New phone number. I might need your help on something."

A meter maid tapped on his windshield and warned him that he needed to move or feed the meter. He pulled away and parked illegally in a back alley, still a mile from his apartment. These kinds of things were never safe to handle at home where Angie could interrupt. He waited while the traffic on the adjacent street filled and then thinned after lunch hour. He still had a bulk of the afternoon before his shift began. Saturday evenings were the busiest time for pizza delivery.

His phone hummed. "What can I do for you?"

A response! What could she do for him! She wanted to know how to make *him* happy. Improve *his* day. Improve *his* life. He reveled at her kindness and looked at the message, much too full of joy to respond. He imagined all the situations she'd present the question while they were together.

After a long day at work.

What can I do for you?

When he was upset.

What can I do for you?

When no one else understood him.

What can I do for you?

He read it until his phone died. On the way home, his cheeks hurt from laughing so hard. He plugged his phone in and devised an answer to her question.

Part 5

Angie snored by Michael's side, her cigarette butt still smoldering in her soda can. He imagined Sarah's body next to him instead. She wouldn't snore or smoke or drink cheap cans of soda before bed without brushing her teeth. He'd never grow tired of touching her.

Michael debated if it was too late to text Sarah. He didn't want to seem creepy. Still, what if she ran into Don tomorrow? The thought sent him into a panic, so exactly two minutes before nine, while cramped in a full-sized bed with his girlfriend, Michael replied.

"Would you be interested in still covering some shifts at your old branch? Sorry for the delay btw."

Nothing. She was out with friends. Just friends. Other females. When his phone finally buzzed, he jumped so hard Angie awoke.

"What are you doing?"

"Go back to sleep," he said. God, the roll of skin on her

back just behind her armpit was repulsive. Sarah was his greatest motivation to escape this one-way relationship. He truly feared Angie's love for him. Her passion. Her anger.

Sarah would be the opposite. Gentle and affectionate. She would never hit him. *What can I do for you?* He waited until Angie's eyes closed to read the message from Sarah.

"I think I could make it work. Obviously, we have the open house this week. I'm pretty booked through Thursday night."

Each thoughtful message became a song to his soul! If Angie woke up again, it would be the fault of his heartbeat.

A quick internet search revealed the branch's open house ran from 4 to 8 on Thursday. He had every right to be in the library that night.

"Wouldn't be until the weekend," he replied.

"Not Friday morning, right? The afterparty might go a little late."

"Oh, that's right. Still not sure if I'm going." Michael's hands were beyond a tremble.

"I thought you were hosting it. Are you not now?"

"I'm kidding." This was difficult.

"Rumor is you're going all out."

He had to set the phone down at this news. He was actually panting. His breathing grew as loud as the snores from the mass next to him. Sarah would be dolled up in a dress, ready to celebrate. He had to be there to protect her from her coworkers. Don would be too occupied, and if she were to get lonely . . .

He thought back to the party he randomly snuck into when he first met Sarah. She wasn't that drunk then, she promised. Their conversation was impeccable as she sat next to him on a couch that sunk inwards, pulling them together. A definite sign from the universe that they were meant to be together. It felt like she loved him back, but before he could confirm it, the host rudely demanded that he leave.

It took him months to find her again on the dating apps, so by the time they reconnected, she had no memory of their initial chat. He'd only changed his name to Brian that time, in case Angie went snooping, but Sarah didn't connect with "Brian" either, so he tried again as Alex. That date didn't even count. She got weird after only a few minutes and left. Beauty has little patience, he told himself when he gave her another chance as Tim. That must have been bad timing. She was clearly upset about something else. The coffee shop was too easy for her to bolt from. The party would be different. He would be different. He would be himself. He would be Michael just like their first encounter. Sarah wouldn't be able to depart so easily this time, nor would she want to.

Part 6

It didn't take long for Don, Sarah, and Helen to puzzle things together. Don suspected something was off about James when he didn't realize he was in a gay bar. Helen apologized to Sarah for giving out her number. Sarah assured them both she wasn't in danger.

"He didn't exactly chase me out of the coffee shop," she said.

Don shook his head. "I just wish there was a way to know who he is."

"*Cruel Interventions*," Helen said.

"I don't follow."

"He checked it out the other day. A charlatan of poetry."

Two things intrigued them after a quick search in the system for his account: first, he returned the books on the same day; second, his name was Michael Stringer, and he lived only a short hike from the Lozano branch. They agreed he would be there Thursday night.

He didn't seem threatening. She wasn't sure why. He obviously cared for her, right? She'd been with enough guys, surviving their crushes, pleas, and demands. Michael (she had to admit she favored that name over the previous aliases) intrigued her in a charming sort of way. Stupid? Maybe. Kinky? A little. Regardless, she could handle herself. It's not like her other relationships were heaven-sent. Physically, the guy wasn't intimidating. If he had plans to hurt her, he would've pulled it off a long time ago. The lonely sap had probably never touched a woman—he wasn't about to harm her.

His home was easy to find after work. A mid-20th-century house sliced into at least four residences with porches and steps merging to a shared walkway from the street. Apartment D's door was off to the side, but the view from her car was protected and clear. She would wait, unsure of her next move. If she needed to confront him tonight, a nosy neighbor would be within earshot.

Was he in there thinking about her? Had he photographed her at work? No wonder she always felt under observation or at least noticed, even during the most minuscule of tasks. Would any of his pictures look good on social media? The situation was almost comical.

When the streetlights overtook the sunset, she considered leaving. Moments later, the door opened. It wasn't him. Instead, a rather sturdy figure appeared. The face was hard to see in the dim light, but the silhouette of the large frame was massive and unmistakably female. A cigarette was lit, and any humor disappeared.

Sarah thought for a moment before digging through her backpack. If Michael was home too, this would be a disaster.

She opened her car door. She'd always been up for taking risks.

Part 7

"I'm going out tonight," Michael said. This statement usually drew less suspicion if he yelled it from another room.

"Where to?" Angie sounded angry.

"An open house. The library reopened, so . . . wanna come?" There was no chance of that happening, but he changed the subject anyway as he neared the door.

"Did you smoke in here today?"

"Better get used to it."

"Why?"

Whenever she "knew" she was right, she paused for an obscene amount of time before answering. "It just so happens that I signed a petition to allow smoking indoors in city businesses."

"What? When?"

"The other night. Some chick had me sign my name, address, number—"

"You're not even a registered voter."

"So."

"So you just gave some stranger your info."

"She wasn't no weirdo."

"They're never going to reverse that law."

"Maybe I will go with you tonight."

If he reacted, she'd suspect something and follow through. "Fine, put something nice on at least."

"How nice?"

"Not those sweats. Or jeans."

"Like . . . a dress?"

He could ride out this bluff as long as he needed to. "Sure. When was the last time you wore a dress?" While

145

Angie pondered this, Michael's thoughts returned to Sarah. She probably wore dresses a few times a week. Sensible ones to work in. Fancy, yet conservative styles for nights like tonight. He bet she had more than one little black dress in her closet. He'd buy her more. He'd buy her everything she wanted. How easy it was to hoard his money from Angie, knowing someday he would spend it on Sarah.

He waited on the couch as his girlfriend lumbered up the steps to her closet. If he left now, would she follow him? If things went as planned, this would be the last night of their relationship anyway. He'd change the locks and spend a week at his parents' house . . . unless things with Sarah happened as quickly as they had with Angie. He'd stay with her. She would protect him from the craziness.

Angie finally folded and spouted a final insult about book nerds, so Michael slipped out the door.

Parking was a mess, but he had all night. He didn't need to see Sarah until the festivities were wrapping up, so over the course of an hour, he positioned his car closer and closer to the branch. And her car. *I'm allowed to be here. I'm allowed to be here.* He took little hops to loosen his adrenaline before entering. "I'm allowed to be here," he whispered as he pulled open the heavy door.

Part 8

Someone was always talking to her. Older couples, especially dirty old men, surrounded her. This didn't upset him too much at first, as it would have looked unorthodox to duck behind the shelves in the distance. The windows were black from nightfall, but for some reason, the lights seemed amplified. He felt exposed. Exposed as her shoulders and the top of her back in the navy blue dress she wore.

The trembling began. If he could maybe talk to

146

someone else. Let her see him. He was worthy of her attention. This encounter could be an accident for her, though destiny for the two of them. He walked by a table and picked up a free pen and some bookmarks.

"Well, hello," Don said.

Michael flinched but recovered with a smile. "Donald, right? Don?"

"Looking for something? Still in search of a job?"

"Anything's better than delivering pizzas," he said. He was doing it. It was a normal conversation. Maybe even a business conversation.

"We've all been there. Who do you deliver for?"

"Lou's," Michael said. "Excuse me. I'm going to get some water." Don was too comfortable. Friendlier than he was after a drink. This worried him.

"We've got punch over this way, you know. See that girl over there in the dress? There's punch and snacks at that table."

The fool had granted him permission to look at Sarah as if she was his! He felt his face flush and suddenly his own cologne burned his nose. Was she aware? He thought he saw her eyes twinkle for him. "I'm not . . . I just . . ."

"Something wrong?"

He shook his head and looked the other way. Twenty minutes until she was free. He'd entered too soon. Don was onto him. He was smiling too much.

Michael walked away and ducked into the nearest restroom. It smelled, but he was finally alone. The minutes passed easily except when he had to pretend to fuss with a contact lens in front of two men. When he emerged a few minutes after eight, guests were gone, tables were removed, and only strangers lingered. He didn't see Sarah . . . or Don. Probably at the afterparty. His steps became bolder, and the trembling had long passed. He was ready to talk to her again. A hello. An apology. Whatever she wanted to talk about.

He considered the night a push. No progress, but he got to see Sarah in a dress. That was worth it. He'd need to explain the cologne to Angie if she was still up.

His eyes adjusted to the darkness as he paced back to his car. It had rained a bit, and his foot splashed a puddle. "Dammit," he said.

A sweet voice spoke. "I know who you are, Michael."

A terrifying ecstasy filled his body.

Part 9

Sarah! He'd forgotten how close her car was. She was sitting in it with her arms resting on the open window. She wore a jacket over her shoulders now and was chewing gum.

"I—I was at the open house," he said. "You looked . . . I just . . ."

"Heard you followed Don the other night."

"He offered me a job. Well, kinda." Were they conversing? She was as friendly as the first time they'd met. "Do you like it here?" He took two steps closer as if approaching an animal that was sure to dash away.

"It's okay." A few more steps. "You shouldn't be out here."

He could lower his voice. "Sarah, we met long ago. Don't you remember?"

She smiled, now perched up in her seat, drawing him closer. "Which time?" A giggle slipped out.

A chance to explain. "Almost a year ago. It was someone's party." Two steps closer.

"Whose?" She was so close.

"I don't know. But we talked and talked."

"Oh, yeah?"

148

She was listening! He walked closer, tiptoeing through verbal land mines. How could he express his love? "I just keep running into you, and I don't know how to . . . how to say how I feel. About you."

She tilted her head to one side, glancing down the street and then back at him. Michael's tunnel vision locked on the girl he'd wanted to have, to possess, for so long. The rest of the city held silent. No sirens or horns, only drizzles of rain landing softly on her cheeks. She was a mythical nymph alone in the city. He was almost within arm's reach now. Her car wasn't even running. Would she take him to the party? Or maybe they could go somewhere alone. His body quivered.

"Are you cold?" she asked.

He nodded yes, knowing she had a solution. More silence. They already had an unspoken language. Their eyes stayed locked as Michael slowly walked around the front of the car. The sweetness of reciprocation intoxicated him. He trembled more but didn't care. Slowly, very slowly, he walked towards the passenger door, like a minute hand on a clock. There was the handle. He took a shaking hand out of his pocket and reached for it.

WHAM! Someone crushed him from the side, and he felt all the joints in his upper body crack like knuckles before he even landed. His hip smashed into the curb while the wind left his lungs. Angie was on top of him, grabbing his collar and shaking him. Beneath her screams, he heard Sarah's car drive away.

Part 10

Angie didn't stick around long enough for him to even press charges, but he called it even when her stuff disappeared by the next afternoon.

His only social interaction was work, where he

eventually increased his hours to five nights a week. Most of the scabs had healed. The one on his lower chin was the most noticeable. People stared but never asked. He hadn't returned to the library. He wasn't sure when he could. He told himself it would be a year before Sarah would give him another chance, or better yet, completely forget about him. He knew he'd visit her from time to time and admire her from afar. Maybe he could leave a note in one of the books being returned.

With his apartment to himself, no one prevented him from printing and hanging pictures of Sarah from her profile. Often, he'd resume the conversation they were having before Angie's interference. She was going to take him home—and then the humiliation. Who would want a man after he'd been crushed into the pavement by a woman? A woman as disgusting as Angie.

As the weeks went on, he let his hair grow out and thicken for the upcoming winter. He tested a beard but didn't like it. Shaving it off only tore a scab from his injury. He'd just have to live with that scar.

On the first snowfall, which was always premature in Chicago, he was finishing up a shift. Each delivery run filled his backseat, and the tippers were generous. One even invited him in for a beer, but he declined in favor of finishing his duty. His next-to-last pizza was in a better neighborhood. A handsome man with sharp eyes in a dress shirt answered after the third time he knocked.

"What's this? I didn't order anything." Michael checked the address on his receipt. The man turned around. "Did you do this?"

"Do this?" Michael said in defense of his pizza. "Sir, it was ordered and paid for ahead of time online to this exact—"

"I did." Sarah appeared behind the man. Her mascara

150

was smeared below her eyes. She wore a t-shirt that stretched down to the middle of her thighs. "I ordered him," she said, wiping her cheeks. "It's been a long time since . . . and there's nothing here for me."

The tears made her eyes brighter, and he thought he saw her smile. Michael nodded. He'd return to the bookshelves tomorrow.

MORE THAN THEY'D SEEN

The first time we saw Mary Jane, she was sitting in the passenger seat of a maroon '81 Camaro outside the Fox Den. The T-tops were off, revealing a mess of dirty blonde hair and tan shoulders. Her sunglasses hid her eyes, but we were already blown away. She was a bedroom poster come to life.

Thomas, the oldest of us by a few years, took the initiative. "Nice wheels," he said.

She smirked and returned her gaze forward as the rest of us pretended to take an interest in the vehicle. I was left holding our faded basketball as my buddy Scott, Thomas's brother, stepped up to the plate. Mary Jane had produced a cigarette seemingly out of thin air, so he offered a light.

"Thank you, young man," she said. Her voice, with a sexy rasp, suggested it wasn't her first Marlboro. I saw Scott glance down at her cleavage as he held the lighter just above it. He was never this smooth.

Just then, the bar door opened, and a man with long

hair and a scowl walked out, followed by a waft of bar stench. The five of us froze as he took in the situation. He lit his cigarette.

"Mary Jane, why are these children bothering you?"

Children. Yes, we were. Or at least I was, still a month away from my thirteenth birthday and the seventh grade. Thomas was the only one to take offense, seeing as how he had a few hairs on his shirtless chest.

"I needed a light, is all," she said. "This little fella was just obliging." There was a twang, which she somehow made exotic in the middle of small-town Indiana. It connected my ears to my heart.

Thomas lingered by the car while the rest of us backed away. He kept his arms folded to make his biceps look bigger. The man didn't seem to even notice him. He let out a small grunt and circled to the driver's side door. Mary Jane exhaled a plume of smoke, and then they were off. A block away at our town's only stoplight, she flicked the last half of the cigarette to the curb and waved back. We stood in wonder.

We waited until the car's deafening engine faded away, and then all began talking at once.

"How old was her boyfriend?"

"Were they just visiting the bar?"

"Who was she waving to?"

"Could Thomas have taken him on?" No, we all agreed, except for Thomas.

"Why was her boyfriend so much older?"

"Because," Roddy said, "chicks like her dig badasses with cars like that. Besides, he wasn't even forty."

"How old was she?"

"Too old for you twerps," Thomas said. "Yep."

"Maybe it was her dad?" Wishful thinking on my part.

Scott took the ball. "Would her dad let her smoke?"

"Or not wear a seatbelt?" Roddy asked.

"She wasn't a kid," I said. We knew every resident in our town and none of them looked like her. We argued the whole walk back to our block agreeing on nothing except Mary Jane was the most beautiful woman we'd ever seen in person.

***

For the next week, anytime we heard an engine it lured us to the streets like a siren's song. We'd all end up lining the street in hopes of another blessing in the form of a Mary Jane appearance. The other boys in the neighborhood heard of our encounter and told tales of their own, and suddenly she was even more topical than the Major League trade deadline.

"I heard her boyfriend plays guitar in a band."

"I heard she's a high school dropout."

"I heard she's got a kid."

"I heard she lives on the top floor of the inn on the square."

"I heard she gets drunk every night at the Fox Den and takes her top off."

Scott, my closest ally, was just as much in love as the rest of us. "Then we need to get into the Fox Den."

"No way," I said. "They'd kick us out before we got through the door." We were playing horse while waiting for the others to show. "But maybe Thomas could get in."

Scott weighed the idea. "He's 18 now, but if he gets in a fight he'd go to the slammer."

"Why would a fight break out?"

Roddy had joined us. "Uh, I don't know, Luke. Uh uh," He loved mocking my voice. "Hey kid, why don't you play a game of eight-ball with my girlfriend and stare at her knockers while she leans over to shoot a combo."

That was my cue to be silent. Once Roddy and the

others joined our group, I was known more for my jumpshot. In this neighborhood of brothers, the bottom of the food chain was my only choice as an only child.

We soaked ourselves in sweat that morning and were about to head out before Thomas made an appearance. "I talked to her," he said. "She was at the Quarter Wash waitin' on her clothes to dry."

I knew the other guys were thinking the same thing as me: underwear, underwear, underwear.

He snorted and looked away. "We chatted quite a bit. Yep."

"Did you find out how old she was?" Scott asked.

Thomas frowned. "You never ask a lady her age." Then he made a five-star production out of lighting a cigarette. I'd never seen him smoke before, but his younger brother bit.

"Since when do you smoke cigs?"

Thomas coughed. "There's a lot of things I do you don't know about, Scotty-boy."

We all smirked. Only Thomas could get away with calling him that. If we strayed from Scott it was as good as ordering a knuckle sandwich.

"You're afraid to go in there," Scott said.

"The Fox Den?"

"I've been in plenty of times," Roddy said.

"Dragging your uncle out doesn't count." Scott returned his stare to his older brother. It was the first time I noticed how tall my best bud was growing. His eyes were now level with Thomas's nose or at least the shadow of whiskers below it.

"What's the wager?" Roddy asked. "Luke, write it down."

Why was I the recordkeeper? No one listened to me.

"If I go into the Fox Den, Scott has to drink a cup of

pond water."

"No way! I'll get worms and be on the can the rest of the summer. Plus you can't just go in there, you have to talk to her."

"How are we going to make sure he does that?" I asked.

"Calling me a liar?" Thomas only bullied me in front of others. Otherwise, we were cool.

I stammered a bit, envious of him getting this opportunity. "Maybe Roddy's uncle could need help again?"

"He's banned. No can do."

We all stood there, desperate for a plan. I think we'd all let Mary Jane absolve us from summertime boredom. Maybe we'd built her up too much. Still, I'd give away two weeks of my allowance for one more glimpse of this mysterious woman.

The idea didn't hit me until our group dissolved for the day. We were on the opposite side of the street from the Fox Den when I saw the same '81 Camaro parked along the street a half block up. "Scott, do we have another basketball?"

"What's wrong with this one?"

I looked at the car. Its T-tops were off. "What if we accidentally . . ."

Scott bit his lower lip and spun the ball in his hands. "It's Thomas's ball. He'd kill me."

"Roddy has a backup. I've got one somewhere that just needs a little air. Plus, it's not like we won't get it back."

"So you just want to throw the ball in the car and you think she'll appear like some genie?"

"We could wait by the car for her to come out. Then we have a reason to talk."

Scott turned his head like he was trying to remember something. Then his eyes grew. "Wait, are you saying you got the hots for her too? You never talk about girls!"

It was true. I kept my hormonal thoughts to myself. I thought I was safe sharing the universal lust for Mary Jane with my best friend. "I'm saying it could lead to one of us getting to talk to her."

"You gotta go in though," Scott said. "No offense, but you still look harmless."

"What?"

"Your voice hasn't changed. You're shorter. I mean, I know we're the same age, but you just look younger."

This wasn't some new realization. I'd been teased that my "balls hadn't dropped yet" all summer anytime my voice cracked. When I lifted my arms on defense, Roddy always asked if I shaved my pits.

"I don't know," I said. "I can't go home smelling like smoke."

"Blame Roddy. Plus Mary Jane's boyfriend already hates me. Probably feels threatened."

I stared at the bar. A real fox den seemed safer. Then I considered the respect I'd gain. "I'll do it." Maybe I'd be the second one to have a real conversation with Mary Jane. Then who would hold court? I'd introduce myself, and she'd call my name out when she passed by our group. The fantasies began to spawn.

"So we put the ball in the car. And why wouldn't we just get it out?"

"We could," I said. "We're just being polite. I don't want to piss that dude off. But maybe we wait until tomorrow?"

"No," Scott crossed the street, ball in hand. "You'll chicken out if it's tomorrow."

I trailed him to the car. Even with the tops open, it released a stench of smoke and cologne. Scott marched directly to the driver's side.

"Bird steps back . . . and drains the jumper!"

I watched as our ball bounced between the steering wheel and the seat for a moment before coming to rest next to the pedals. "Your turn," he said. "Better get in there before all the regulars."

Normally I would be terrified to cross into somewhere forbidden, but the need to see Mary Jane outweighed any fear. I pushed the door at first, then realized I had to pull before entering. It was dark and the haze clung to me instantly. I felt invisible. A man's laughter erupted at the end of the bar, but it wasn't at me, or anything. Is this what drunks did all day? Amuse themselves, glass after glass? Mary Jane deserved a better life than this.

"All right, whose rugrat is here to pick 'em up?" a lady called out. She had the petite figure of a college girl, but her face looked fifty.

"I just need some help," I said.

"Speak up, pipsqueak," she said.

"My ball fell into the car outside, and I—"

"What are you talking about?"

Meek wouldn't cut it. "Who owns the Camaro?"

She turned away. "Stan! Someone hit your car."

Why had I volunteered for this? Roddy was more prepared for this mission. Or even Scott. I wondered if my friend would be outside for support or if he'd already fled far enough to spy from a distance.

"Stan? You back there?"

"Ma'am, no one hit his car. *No one hit his car!*"

She smirked at me and laughed before a man came out. "There ya are."

He was the same guy who called us all children. He strode through the bar, leaving a swinging door behind him. I glanced around the joint for another exit. There was an employee-only door to the side of the bar and two doors for restrooms at the opposite end. Moments later, Stan returned with our basketball in his hands. Somehow, he was still oblivious to me as he walked over to a booth I couldn't see into and set it there.

"Here. Present." I cowered as he turned back toward me. If only I could've remained unnoticed for a few more seconds.

"What the hell are you doing in my bar, kid?"

"That was my ball. Thanks for getting it. I didn't want to—"

"You got about three seconds to get the hell out of here or I'll toss your ass out myself."

"Yes, sir, leaving now."

"Ha! I like being called sir."

"He called me ma'am!" the lady yelled.

Had I just saved myself? "Sir, I apologize once again. It wasn't my fault. Can I please have my ball back please?" I sounded like a baby.

I looked towards the booth where he'd placed it. Right then, Mary Jane peered around the side at me. Suddenly, this deadly mission seemed worth it. She smiled, and I saw her without sunglasses. What a face with eyeshadow and long lashes like an actress!

"Git!" Stan yelled. I ran out of the bar to echoes of laughter.

My friend was no comfort. "You didn't get it back? Thomas is going to kill me. I'm telling him. I have to."

"It wasn't my fault." I wanted to tell him about Mary Jane and the way she smiled at me, but he was too mad. I'd cherish that moment while I could. "I'll find a way to get it back. I promise. Just tell Thomas I borrowed it and you left before me."

"I can't believe you thought this would work."

In my mind, it had.

That night, I still didn't have a plan to retrieve Thomas's

basketball, but I knew sitting at home wouldn't resolve anything. The sun had already set when I positioned myself across the street from the Fox Den. Every so often, a patron would enter through the doorway. I didn't know what miracle I expected. Best-case scenario? Mary Jane would stroll out with a smile and our ball, and then she would suggest we work on free throws until sunrise.

A layer of clouds buried the last of the sunset, and the street lights flickered on. I ignored the universal curfew. I was turning 13 soon, so why did that kiddy rule still apply to me? Roddy and Scott never fled home. And maybe if I got in trouble, it would stall Thomas's persecution. Further up the street, I spotted the Camaro.

It started to sprinkle, and I became more self-conscious. Someone in the bar would spot me, perhaps Stan or that loud bartender lady. I paced further south for a block and then crossed the street. I'd make one final pass at the Fox Den. Maybe I'd get lucky, and a friendly drunk would walk out around then. I could ask him if there was a basketball lying around. He'd smile and check for me. I'd return it to Scott's house that night, and all would be well.

None of that happened.

When I walked past the Fox Den, its door remained shut. The smoke stench took me back to earlier in the day when our plan took a left turn. I sped by afraid of Stan, however, I did notice how loud it was inside. A crowd and a distorted jukebox tune, something country, blasted through the walls. I said a small prayer as I neared Stan's car. He'd wisely replaced the T-tops before the rain. I made a quick pass but couldn't find the courage to search for my ball. The bar's door swung open, so I jetted across the street. No one came out. I stood in the shadows in front of the hardware store. I'd wait and see if the car was unlocked like everyone else's in town. If the ball was in there, it would only take me a moment. I could outrun chain-smoker Stan for three blocks to the police station. They'd have to protect me. I'm a boy with a ball!

A few mosquitoes who'd also taken shelter under the awning found my neck. I'd waited long enough; it was now or never.

Wanting to look less suspicious, I walked. I'd try the driver's side door, then the passenger side. My heart raced as I crossed the street diagonally. Before I reached the curb, the door to the Fox Den opened again. A figure emerged. The cherry of his cigarette told me all I needed to know, so I immediately b-lined back toward the hardware store. I glanced over my shoulder, relieved he hadn't acknowledged me. I stepped into the doorway and pinned myself to the darkest corner.

Stan fumbled his keys before entering the Camaro and driving off.

Defeated, I stepped back into the middle of the lifeless street, not far from where the car had been parked. Was our ball traveling further away?

I stood with my hands on my hips with a plan B which was based on the lingering rumors. Up the street, the Market Square Inn was the only sign of life. The old building was known for its vintage sign from when it opened some six decades ago before the Great Depression. Our town's only landmark, we visited it on a field trip in second grade. Even then, a bunch of old rooms and furniture wasn't anything we considered noteworthy. My only memory was seeing our town from the top floor. A new perspective of somewhere so familiar. I began walking toward the glowing sign and stopped just across the street from it.

I looked up to the third-story windows. The white bulbs of the sign gently illuminated the top of the building. A figure stood between the barely opened curtains. Like an illusion or an angel, Mary Jane looked down, but not at me. She was standing in her underwear. I can't say how long either of us stood there, me in the street, her between curtains, but I would have remained forever. And then the curtains closed.

I could barely get my legs to move. Finally, I backtracked toward the hardware store. The basketball was no longer a priority. I'd forgotten all about it. What did any of this mean?

I retreated home empty-handed but completely in love.

The next day, I planned on staying home to avoid Thomas. I was content to lie around until nightfall before venturing into town and setting up camp in hopes of another private encounter with the goddess from above. I decided Mary Jane had indeed seen me. She knew who came to retrieve the basketball she'd cradled probably moments before. *Come and get it,* she was saying. *It'll be our little secret, Luke.* My childhood ended that afternoon as I fantasized about the possibilities. I began to do the math. If she was only eight years older than me, by the time I graduated high school, she'd only be 26. That wasn't a big deal. We'd become special friends in the meantime. The neighborhood would worship me. Whose balls had dropped now?

The afternoon dragged on until my mother pestered me into chores. Anything to pass the time. I once heard that the hands of a clock don't move swiftly for a man in love. That's what I was now: A man. In love.

It was almost time for supper when Scott found me in the backyard. "You won't believe what happened. Come over, you gotta hear this!"

I skipped permission and raced to my buddy's yard. "Wait, is this a trap?"

"No, Thomas ain't mad. He got the ball back!"

I'd never seen my friend so excited. Maybe I could share my secret with him.

Brothers galore gathered on the patio. We could have drafted an 11-on-11 football game with the amount of sweaty, shirtless, skinned-up-knee boys sitting around. To the side of the house, Thomas finished washing his dad's Chrysler and then walked around carrying the hose. "Jesus, Scotty, did you tell the whole neighborhood?"

Obviously, but what was the point? Part of me wanted to spill everything. But it was our moment. For the rest of my life I would remember that vision. And would they even believe me? No, I'd contain myself and see what Thomas knew. Maybe he got into it with Stan and won his ball back.

Thomas scanned his congregation. "Anyone got a smoke?"

Roddy, who never shared, quickly provided and then stayed quiet for the first time in his life, which concerned me. That's when I spotted the ball next to the step by the backdoor. A sense of relief washed over me.

"So yeah, Saturday night, I don't want any of your twerps hanging around the Magic Freeze, got it?"

Roddy nodded his head. "Tell 'em why, Tommy!" He was never this positive.

"I'm taking Mary Jane for sundaes."

Some of the boys whooped and cheered, some yelled out things about banana splits. My heart crumbled. Tears welled up, and I had to turn away and duck behind the crowd. I had never felt the terror of jealousy in my life. How easily could it have been me to retrieve that ball and get a chance? Why had I run away like a coward? I'd never forgive myself.

"All I had to do was go to the Fox Den when they opened at lunch and ask for my ball back, and there she was, pretty as hell, by the way, and she gave it to me."

"Wasn't her boyfriend there?" someone asked. Thomas waved the question off. "That dude ain't even her boyfriend. That's her old man."

I'd concluded this earlier. Or at least assumed she was unhappy and lonely, boyfriend or not. A satisfied girlfriend doesn't stand in her bra and panties in a window. Plus, Stan looked a decade older in the rain and darkness than he did at our first encounter. A father for sure. And probably one tired of fending off bums like Thomas.

"So yeah, I just told her I owed her a favor and said ice cream was on me tomorrow. That simple. Yep."

The chit-chat resumed as a pit formed in my stomach. Scenarios circulated. He could take her to ice cream, but I'd still be her audience outside that window. Maybe there was a pattern. A phase of the moon, or if the air was just right, I'd grow an instinct and know when it was time for her to appear. We'd leave notes for each other. She'd finally come down and talk about her problems with Thomas and how she couldn't stand how he always said "yep" after everything. She'd playfully tap my shoulder, I'd tap hers back, and then somehow we'd be holding hands in the silence of Market Square.

"So is she going to high school here now?" Roddy asked. The crowd groaned. To mention school in July was blasphemous.

"Doubt it," Thomas said. He folded his arms, smug as ever. "Any other issues I should inquire about?"

"Where does she—"

"Not really, you twerps. From here on out, you can mind your own business and stay clear tomorrow night. Got it?" He walked over and picked up the basketball and then glared in my direction.

He'd forgiven me, but I would *never* forgive him.

So, of course, we went to the Magic Freeze that next evening. Not actually to it, but to the bike trail at the edge of town, a stone's throw away. I hadn't ridden my bike all summer, or even for the last year. I'd outgrown it but didn't have the cash for a ten-speed, so when I pedaled, my knees bumped the handlebars. Roddy was in the same conundrum and was even taller than me. A few other boys showed up, and we laughed at our unplanned rendezvous and what a coincidence it was that we all just felt like using the old bike trail on a Saturday night. Scott must have known better because he stayed home.

Our view was unobstructed. Too unobstructed. Had Thomas pulled up, he would've spotted the half-dozen of us staked out. I suggested we stash our bikes in the thin patch of woods nearby.

"Nah, too far," said Roddy. "I have a better plan."

"But Thomas said—"

"What's he gonna do to me?" asked Roddy. "You think I'm scared of him? Besides, we have as much right to be there as he does."

I considered his logic. Since Roddy was our next in command, he could take the brunt of Thomas's wrath. And maybe he was right. Could Thomas still beat up the freckly, crooked-toothed pal of ours? Roddy was an enigma to me. All I knew was that my mother "preferred he not come over."

"What if we got ice cream to go?" I asked.

Roddy gave me a look of approval for the first time in my young life. "We take our time ordering in the front window. Maybe ask for extra nuts or if got have any new flavors. Meanwhile, those two come walking by. Thomas gives us a dirty look, but so what? He's the one with something at stake, not us, right?"

The other boys looked to me for confirmation, but I

was sold. Convinced of the connection Mary Jane and I already had, it was a chance for me to lay more groundwork. She'd recognize me, and through some method—a smile, a wink, a whisper—she'd invite me back to the street for another show.

"Anyone know what time they were heading here?" Roddy asked. None of us wore a watch.

"When I left, his car was still in the driveway," I said. "The bank clock said it was a quarter after seven on my way here."

Roddy grumbled and then started pedaling toward the intersection. "Let's just hang out front then."

We followed, our legs pumping hard to keep up. Roddy dropped his bike on the faded lines near the handicapped parking, so we did the same, leaving a pile of Huffys. Three of the four picnic tables were taken, but we squeezed into one on the end. No one said anything as we quietly waited, craning our necks anytime a car approached.

Eventually, a manager not much older than Roddy came out. "You fellas have to order something or leave. These tables are for paying customers."

"We're waiting on our girlfriends," Roddy said. "It's rude getting a head start. Right, Miss?"

The rest of us couldn't keep it together. No way this girl believed any of us chumps had girlfriends. Roddy dropped his head as we laughed.

"Fine, fine. We'll order," Roddy said. Like a trained army, we followed him to the window. I couldn't tell what he ordered, but it was presented to him in a small Styrofoam cup. Same with the next few fellas.

I was last and, of course, penniless. "I'll just have a water."

"Gina, all five of these little turds ordered water," the manager from earlier said across the window. "Look, we're happy to have your business when you order something, but there are water fountains elsewhere. You got faucets at home, right?"

I nodded with shame. Then the sliding window slammed shut. "Looks like you should've gone first," Roddy said.

I didn't acknowledge him. The car I'd seen a million times in our neighboring driveway had already parked. Thomas was opening the door, and I'm certain that if I had a cup to hold, I would've dropped it.

Mary Jane was a movie star. Her hair was a messy bunch of pinned-up curls. Her sunglasses stole half of her face, but she had the impossible figure and proportions of one of those cartoon characters we boys always felt awkward about being attracted to. Her legs stemmed out from her cutoff jean shorts, and even her hamstrings were defined. She wore sandals with a modest heel, although none of that was noticeable compared to her chest. The five of us must have looked like a crowd of hypnotized maniacs, but we didn't care. The moment we'd been waiting for all summer strutted past us.

To my disappointment, Mary Jane didn't acknowledge me. Thomas opened the door for her and then turned back to us and mouthed, "All of you, dead!"

"Worth it," Roddy said, arms folded. "Well worth it. And he won't do nothing. Let's go."

Reluctantly, I followed my gang back to the bike trail. We chatted for a bit about the sight we'd just seen and speculated how badly Thomas would screw it up.

"The way she just . . . the curves on that broad!" Roddy bit his fist. "I guess we should get going and not press our luck with Loverboy just in case. Maybe he'll bring her around us soon enough."

That would be incredible, we concluded. We said our

goodbyes, and then no one left. We all grabbed our bikes, but Roddy tied a shoelace, Mickey loped over to the woods to take a leak, and I didn't even pretend I was about to leave.

"How long's it take to eat ice cream?" I asked. The answer was 38 minutes. We watched again as Thomas paraded Mary Jane back to the car. Her sunglasses were off, and even though it was distant, I felt eye contact.

"They ain't holding hands," Roddy said. "He screwed up. Probably didn't pay for hers, the cheapskate that he is."

"Or she just doesn't like him," I said. "Why would she go out with a guy still in high school, right?" I looked for reassurance, but everyone else was still enraptured.

When the car finally pulled away, we were all thinking the same thing: When was our next chance to lay eyes on Mary Jane?

Thomas told us nothing. For a week, we barely saw him. He picked up a job at the lumber yard and stopped making appearances at the courts.

Scott was no help. "He won't tell me a thing about her!"

"Did they hold hands? Did he get to first base? Are they going out again?"

"Hell if I know!" It was his answer to everything, no matter how many times we asked. There weren't even any repercussions for our little intrusion of the date, although we gladly would have suffered just for a speck of knowledge about Mary Jane.

"Something must be wrong with her," Roddy finally decided.

"No way," I said. "Thomas messed it up by taking her to ice cream instead of dinner."

"She looked happy," Roddy said. "Maybe they had dinner there. The burgers and fries aren't bad. Or so I've heard. I give the water four stars."

"Too bad she doesn't have any sisters," I said.

Everyone looked at me. I blushed. Roddy walked over and put his arm around my shoulder. "Look whose balls must've finally dropped. Congratulations, kid."

I shook loose of his embrace as everyone laughed. What did they know? Just because I didn't spout crude remarks and draw genitals in bathroom stalls didn't mean I wasn't becoming a man.

More days passed, and summer began to deflate much like our basketball. Back-to-school signs popped up in the stores. The sun set earlier. Our routines grew old.

One Saturday morning, Thomas finally appeared at a pickup game. When he arrived, Roddy made a face at me as if to suggest I should ask him. I shook it off. Breaking the ice was number two's job, not mine.

"So where ya been, Tommy baby?"

"Working. You should try it sometime. Might be able to afford to trim that carrot top of yours."

Someone missed a shot, but no one scrambled for the rebound. "Okay, okay. Let's not beat around the bush, Casanova. Tell us what happened."

I held my breath and glanced at Scott. Was this the day Roddy took over as our alpha? We all knew he no longer feared Thomas. Maybe Thomas sensed it too.

He shrugged a bit. "Just didn't work out. Nice girl, yep. Er, lady, I guess. Something just wasn't right. Know what I mean?"

None of us did, but Roddy seemed to soften. "That's too bad." Someone finally retrieved the ball and took another shot. "Any chance we see her in the hallways? Maybe you sit by her in math and give it another shot for homecoming?"

Thomas shook his head no, and that's when we all came to the same conclusion. She wasn't in high school. She wasn't impressed by the starting quarterback. She wouldn't be fawning in the bleachers like the other girls he had his pick of. Roddy picked up on this too, and when Thomas turned his back, he made a funny face. We all owed him one for the grilling.

Thomas's melancholy rubbed off on everyone else that afternoon. Except I was faking it. Inside, my heart jumped for joy, and my play reflected it. I couldn't miss! Even Roddy high-fived me after my third straight jumper.

That night, I had the confidence of a warrior. As the sun began to set, I grabbed my own sun-stained basketball and dribbled into town. I didn't fear Stan anymore. If he let his daughter go out with Thomas, what threat was I? I detoured a bit to set up the longest walk past Market Square and the inn. How many nights had I missed Mary Jane coming to the window? Admittedly, not so many. Once or twice a week, I still allowed myself to be lured into a stroll past that portal of a third-story window, but she never appeared. One night, a policeman even asked what I was doing. But, it was one of those lucky days when I couldn't miss a jump shot, so why not ride this hot streak out?

I dribbled as loudly as I could. Nothing. I continued to the empty courts but struggled to resume my sharpshooting from earlier in the day. Who cared? I wasn't there to practice; the whole trip was just a lottery ticket to see her.

A bad miss caused my ball to roll into a mud puddle that never seemed to evaporate. Why wasn't there anyone else for me in this stupid town? What was in the water preventing anyone in our neighborhood from having a sister? No wonder we all fell in love with Mary Jane. She was the beautiful world none of us had access to and probably never would.

The heat lightning on the horizon appeared closer. For all I cared, it could strike me dead. What would it matter?

At least she'd hear about me then. "Oh, that poor boy," she would say while reading the newspaper. "I sure do remember him fondly."

The clouds moved in, and it began to sprinkle. Speckled drops at first. The ball got a little slick, but the rain felt good. Steam rose off the baked pavement, releasing the scent that sticks with someone like an early childhood memory.

As the rain increased, shooting around felt ridiculous. I was already a shoo-in to start on the seventh-grade team, and being out in the rain would only garner questions from my parents. At least there was hope as I got to pass by that fateful spot one more time on the journey home.

I locked my eyes on the window as soon as it was in view. Was there a light on? Were the curtains open? The streetlight a half-block away wasn't doing me any favors. The downpour increased as I sheltered in the hardware store doorway. An excuse to set up camp. Even a police officer would understand.

I perched a seat on the ball and leaned forward, gazing through the rain at the dark window. The bank clock said 8:55. I'd give it until 9:00 which was technically my curfew.

Okay, 9:03, then I would go home. 9:05. 9:10 was a round number.

Nothing but darkness, and I hadn't even noticed the rain stopped. My excuse now absent, I headed home, scolding myself for being so pathetic. I walked directly through puddles as punishment. I'd be alone in this town until I was a hundred. I was sure of it.

Three blocks further, as I was about to turn onto my street, I heard the familiar roar of an engine rapidly approaching. Sure enough, it was Stan's Camaro that sped right past me. I was splashed right at the crotch of my shorts. I didn't know if Mary Jane was on board. Had her father left her at home? Was she as lonely as me?

I raced back. Why hadn't I waited until 9:30? Had I missed him dropping her off? *You impatient idiot!* I must have looked like a madman bouncing my ball through the soaked sidewalks of our desolate town. But when I got back to my spot, her window was still dark.

My clothes were drenched, and my shoes would need a full day to dry. I was sure to catch hell from Mom for being out so late, and for what? What was wrong with me? What did I think was going to happen? I began to question if the window incident was even real. The mind of a teenage boy is driven by one thing. Maybe they left out some details about hallucinating in health class. Did I really think a woman who wasn't even impressed by Thomas wanted anything to do with me?

I had no explanation for my parents when I got home. "You'll be home by seven sharp the rest of this summer," Mom stated. She piled on chores and berated me with questions I couldn't answer.

Ugh, the dreaded weeks of August. They felt like waiting in a doctor's office. Boredom combined with the desire to just get it over with. I tried to look forward to autumn: the beginning of football season, the harvest carnival, and my first day of junior high.

I had it all during that one summer night. I should've run into the street, gotten down on one knee, and professed my love to the goddess above me . . . if it even happened. How could a woman I'd only seen a handful of times steal my heart so quickly? How did the rest of the crew not feel this way?

During our final week of summer freedom, I noticed Mary Jane's name didn't come up once. I knew we all still thought about her, but we'd established a silent agreement. A truce to subdue our love for her. Maybe next summer she would return. I could grow a foot in that year and sprout some facial hair. My voice would deepen, and I could look the other guys in the eye without craning my neck.

The fateful day arrived like an unwelcome relative. Begrudgingly, we all put on the long pants and new shirts that our mothers said made us look like fine young men and trudged to school.

I'd memorized my schedule but still uncrumpled it to make sure I should start my day in room 15. An enthusiastic teacher with a mustache welcomed us in and told us to sit anywhere. I wouldn't see Scott until third hour, so I dropped into a chair in the fourth row before opening my trapper.

I readjusted myself in my stiff blue jeans as the bell rang. A few more students scrambled in, and one took the seat to my right.

"Please get out a pencil," the teacher said. "You'll all need to fill out this form I'm handing out."

A faint smell of cigarette smoke caught my attention. I looked over and saw God's display of perfection sitting right next to me. "Hey, do you have a pencil?" Mary Jane asked.

"Yeah," I said, my voice now an octave lower.

Poetry

I learned to write poetry from the late Dr. David Citino, a professor at Ohio State. "Often Me" is a poem we workshopped in his class while the other two were written later in life. They're just as personal as some of the short stories.

Before Sex

Before sex the best feeling in the world was an open field you could sprint through forever,
It was a secret hiding place even when no one was looking for you,
It was peeling the foil wrapper off and taking the first bite,
It was hours into a video game and reaching a new level while your little brother cheered you on,
It was staying up late at your friend's house trading secrets before falling asleep on the floor,
It was opening a Happy Meal and finally getting the elusive toy to the collection.
Before sex, the best feeling was a blank page and a fresh box of 64 Crayolas that didn't need sharpening, but you did it anyway because you could,
It was the entrance gate to the zoo with the smell of elephants in the distance,
It was the rare occasion you drank soda fizzing from a two-liter and you got your refill before it ran out,
It was a basketball court all to yourself and the swish that was always louder when no one else was around.
Before sex the best feeling was a chain restaurant after you'd graduated from the kids' menu, but you could still get french fries,
It was Mom reading you a book for the first time, and then dozens of times after that,
It was playground equipment at your cousin's school that was so much better than yours,

It was your fourth-grade teacher's science experiment that blew your mind,
It was the trailer for the sequel of a movie you loved,
It was when your favorite song came on in the car even though you had to hide your joy from your older sibling,
It was the smell of charcoal Dad just lit for the picnic while you counted to ten behind a tree pretending your eyes were closed,
It was leaving your jacket on at school because you were about to leave for a field trip,
It was the lifeguard's whistle when adult swim was over,
It was the first tee at putt-putt,
It was five minutes till seven on Christmas morning,
It was finding out that she liked you even though you barely knew each other,
And then you go and fall in love,
And ruin it.

Why Teachers Laugh at Their Own Jokes

I laugh at my own jokes because
despite what I said,
I'd probably get fired
for what's really in my head.

Don't judge me for the jokes I crack
to survive another day,
Being professional means censoring
what I really want to say.

If I was always serious
this class would be a big bore,
I'd be just another teacher
and one you would ignore.

Before I got hired here,
my whole career was on stage,
And even though I love this job
it can still feel like a cage.

I laugh at my own jokes
and wear these happy faces
Even while I lose patience
on a regular daily basis.

Did you guys hear the one about the teacher
who tried to do his best?
No, 'cause had your earbuds in
while I was telling you about the test.

"Gees Durham, was that a dad joke?
You don't even have a kid.
Don't you believe in reproducing?"
Well maybe once we did.

But he arrived 4 months too early,
but nobody ever knew,
'Cause I showed up the next day to teach
just like I always do.

"Oh, whoops, so sorry,
ever thought about adoption?"
Yes, it's expensive,
so I chose another option.

To put my focus on you
so my effort's always legit,
Instead of changing diapers,
I'll put up with all your shit.

So before you start mocking me,
let me tell you what else is true,
I have to laugh at myself
because I'm not allowed to laugh at you.

Often Me

Can't scare away the past
so it lasts like winter. Saw my
shadow in the alley's slush
while my friends ran away
with their lovers like the dish
and its spoon, with noodles eaten
three nights in a row plus a lonely
lunch with leftovers from that which
was left behind. Efforts dried up
like the crumbs that roll under the fridge,
covered by the same hum
of visits like a favorite bridge
that still can't get the simple
points across while time flows
like the water beneath it—hitting
the smooth rocks just right so no one
feels hurt until it's gone.

Like the last time love left, leaving smoke
and exhaustion because I could never sleep
on her ideas. Too late now, you are who you
are and who you aren't with is someone else.
Tried so hard to avoid the puddles
in a dirty personality and no matter
how much soap is added, no one is there
to rinse, just repeat like a chorus of
relationships ending on low notes. So I keep

their pictures pretending like I mattered
to them, but still won't until much later.
When we all get sick of being our unselves
we'll learn not to throw away what
attracted them just to please while
losing more than religion. Sunday
had not come in a while, but evening
sure knew how to keep the door closed
with a tiny lock that could be broken
if anyone tried hard enough.

Attempting to change the color
of lonely to love or find the prism
of my emotion from unsad or gray
like father's hair when he can't teach
with shortcuts anymore. Lessons
as invisible as the blue clouds
in the seasons of the sky's prime
of those days I can't relive
when I had too much time
to think and realize that
no one worthwhile is ever easy,
except me.

Creative Nonfiction

"Crutch" is a piece I originally wrote for a show called *Listen to Your Mother* in 2015 (which has since been rebranded as *Mama Said, Mama Said*). I share it with my students every year because it's the best advice my mother ever gave me.

"Why I'm a Bears Fan" started as a Facebook post. After workshopping it, I realized there was much more to it. It describes how I overcame a hardship in my late twenties and my connection with the heartbreaking Chicago Bears.

"Forgive the Teenager" also began as a Facebook post and turned into my second participation in the *Mama Said, Mama Said* St. Louis show. So many important people in my life never got to meet my mother. This essay personifies her very well.

CRUTCH

Cling, clang, clang, cling, clang. Growing up it was often my job to set the table for the five of us. First the forks, then the spoons; we shared a butter knife. Five places, five sounds. *Cling, clang, clang, cling, clang* rang out over our dark brown antique kitchen table that my mother, father, older sister, and younger brother shared every night.

When I was thirteen my mother was diagnosed with breast cancer. The news ended my childhood. Two years later, after all of the surgery, after all of the chemotherapy, after all of the radiation, after all of the weight loss and hair loss, she called me downstairs to tell me the cancer had spread to her brain and she was dying. As a fifteen-year-old momma's boy, I threw myself to the worn living room carpet and said, "Then I don't want to live either." The words came out even before the tears which soon followed. Certainly God would change his mind now.

Mom exhaled a small laugh and with her bony hand, lightly patted the spot on the couch next to her. She wiped a few of my tears away like she did when I was a child, but I didn't stop crying. "I want you to remember something," she said. "Even though you're going to lose me, you don't ever get to use that as a crutch." Her voice was firm but comforting.

I didn't know what she meant. I had a two-week experience with crutches at the end of my seventh-grade year when my left leg experienced severe growing pains, but this was different.

"A crutch," she went on, "is an excuse to stop trying. To stop taking care of yourself. To stop living. A lot of times when something goes wrong in a person's life, especially a kid, they stop caring about everything else and use the tragedy as an excuse to fail." She put her arm around me. "You won't do that."

I reflected back on my track meet earlier that week when I almost gave up halfway through a race, finishing in last place before going under the bleachers and crying, but this wasn't the same thing. Or was it? I knew my coach would understand my poor performance if I explained. Everyone knew what I was going through, so my failure was excused. It was so easy to lean on my sadness. Could she blame me?

Mom reiterated, "You never get to use my death as an excuse for yourself or your efforts for anything in life."

As soon as she passed away, it made sense even more. The opportunities to fail were everywhere, and everyone would have understood. Everyone except her.

If only other kids who endured a loss or a hardship could have heard her message. How different would the universal stages of death be for them? The anger, the guilt, the time before acceptance—which never seems permanent anyway. How many people take the easy way out of life's low points and the crosses they have to bear, or the inevitable pains that grab them by the soul, because God clearly doesn't care anyway, so what's the point?

Obviously her message stuck with me. I share it with each of the high school classes I teach when we're going through some sort of emotional friction as a group. I try to imagine what conflicts my students are encountering, and how her talk with me can help them through it. I think back to my teenage years after Mom died, when we had to get used to sitting down at the kitchen table where there was now an empty seat. We had to learn to find the joys in life again and continue on with our daily tasks as a family of four.

Cling, clang, clang, cling.

WHY I'M A BEARS FAN

The first time I walked into Soldier Field, my breath ran ahead of me, squeezing my lungs like a relative hugging me too hard. The painted gridiron I had seen so many times on television—it was right there. It was the set of my favorite movie or like walking through a chapter of my favorite book. Orange and blue, the colors that always grab my attention when together, were everywhere. At last, I was surrounded by people with the same passion for the Chicago Bears. My eyes welled up, as I began to weep. I ducked into a restroom, and a tear streaked down my face like a Devin Hester punt return.

I was 39 years old.

At eight I didn't watch much of the NFL, until one Sunday Dad asked, "Who do you want to win, the Bears or the Rams?" I said the Bears. They did and then crushed the Patriots to win Super Bowl XX. After a stream of player endorsement deals, Saturday Night Live skits, and even a music video, the '85 Bears became part of American pop culture and my favorite team. Not my parents', not my siblings', or buddies', just mine. Why weren't they everyone's favorite team? They were the greatest right then, but I had no idea my heart was signing a life-long contract.

Every autumn, whether the Bears were on that week or not, Dad and I sat on our worn couch to watch football. The shift of the fall sun did more than cool off the Sunday afternoons. By mid-October, a glare would drag its way across our television screen. It arrived near the end of the first quarter and lasted until late into the second half. Finally, I grew tall enough to drape an afghan across the curtain rod so that only specks of light would pollute the screen. Instead of getting worked up about a game, Dad would lie on the couch, and I would sit across his legs near the armrest. After answering my questions about a rule or a player--or maybe sharing an anecdote about a historical game, he would catch a quick nap. When he woke up and games got close, I knelt by the television serving as the remote.

"Change it to four. Now six, nope commercial--back to four." There was no internet, and highlights weren't readily available. Instead, I was at the mercy of NBC's Ten-Minute Ticker to update me on the Bears' score while Dad focused on his Browns.

For Christmas, my parents bought me a Bears mini-football which my friends and I wore out at recess. Over the years other gifts followed: T-shirts, stickers, hats, posters, mugs, a blanket, a throw pillow (which is still often thrown during games), and other meaningful collectibles.

When I was 15, my mother gave me a Bears sock hat. It's fuzzy and worn out now, but it stays ready in my closet. She bought it in Chicago while she was there for cancer treatments. It was her final gift to me.

In college, my best friend Eric, who became a Bears fan later in childhood, was able to get a framed, autographed Mike Singletary picture for me. He worked security at a signing in Chicago and knew how much it would mean to me because I tried to get Singletary's autograph before a game at Cleveland when I was a kid, but the hall-of-fame linebacker didn't stop. Eric also gave me a Curtis Conway jersey. Out of all of their terrible first-round selections, Conway is one of the worst. Still, it's my only Bears jersey, so I've worn it to every Bears game that I've attended. "Conway? That's a blast from the past," fellow Bears fans always say. A true fan would remember him, and a true fan still wears the jersey because it brings luck.

While living in St. Louis, I went alone to every single Bears game when they were in town against the Rams. I would always get on the Metrolink, proudly sporting my Conway jersey, an alien in dark blue and orange among a crowd of glaring Rams gold. I was taunted with snickers and boos, and one time even a deaf guy harassed me through sign language. But on the ride back from the stadium that night, no one said a thing. Just like when I was eight, the Bears beat the Rams.

Football seasons can mimic life in how the good times come and go. There are pathetic years, there are landmark years, but unless the season ends with a Super Bowl victory, ultimately there is a letdown. The 2006-07 season was one where Sunday afternoons became the only positive part of my week as the Bears won their first eight games. For three hours, I could forget that I was in an awful relationship sharing an awful apartment with a few awful months left on a lease. And as the Bears clinched home-field advantage through the playoffs, I could forget the previous seasons of disappointment. It was like I was eight again.

Even though they were playing in it, I declined Super Bowl party invitations because it was a game I needed to watch alone. I bought a six-pack and a bag of chips and stayed home. Even the introduction to the game led to a swell of emotions for everything this team meant to me. All of the teasing I endured in the miserable 90s during high school dripped off my face. The worthless years of mediocrity when someone else was crowned champion could be forgotten. How could I have possibly known what a Super Bowl win meant when I was a child? Now it would mean everything. Could life at least give me that?

The Bears returned the opening kickoff for a touchdown and the game stayed close. Five beers later in the second half, as the Bears' deficit grew after Rex Grossman threw a pick-six, I had to admit the dream season was ending. My current relationship needed to end as well. I called my employee helpline for counseling and said, "I need to see someone. The only good thing in my life is losing the Super Bowl. Everything else is a mess."

"How's Thursday at six work?"

The relationship and the lease concluded a few months later at the end of April. I had a lot to pack and move into my own place. In the back of the fridge, I found the last beer from that lonely six-pack that I never finished, so I swallowed the bitterness of the loss once more. But the NFL draft was that same weekend, and it promised a new class of rookies and hope. I resumed packing my possessions for my new home. Buried in the bottom of my closet, beneath the piles of clothes, its fuzzy orange and blue threads barely holding on, was my Bears sock hat. It was warm on that first day of May, but I put it on anyway and finished carrying my stuff out.

That summer I debated moving away from St. Louis, but I met a girl across the river in Illinois. Within minutes I knew that I would love her. I can't explain why. On our first real date, I asked her, "Do you root for the Bears or the Rams?"

"The Bears. Of course."

My heart signed another life-long contract. Two years later we married on the first day of May.

FORGIVE THE TEENAGER

It was Christmas Eve, and I was about to switch off the lights on our pre-lit tree for the night. For the last two years, there's been a noticeable gap of darkness where a strand of lights went out—leaving a one-foot void in the middle. However, for one moment—that gap had a half-dozen lights shining with twice the intensity. It was eerie how much brighter they glowed, almost like stars. They didn't stay lit very long. Moments later, they went out to create the division of the upper and lower half of the tree like before.

I don't think they were one of those supernatural signs from my mother. She doesn't send signs other than showing up in dreams near my birthday. But, I was thinking about her. The last time my Mom was alive for Christmas, I was only 15. Her birthday falls on December

27, and she would've been 74. Her hair would be completely gray by now.

She didn't have much hair when she died, but I do remember a moment a few weeks after she had finished a series of chemotherapy treatments when her hair began growing back. We were on the front porch, and while I was in a mild panic that my peers might walk by and see my nearly bald mother, she held up a hand. Her eyes were closed and a few tears ran down her face. "I can feel the wind in my hair," she said. "I haven't felt that in so long." I wish I had been old enough to understand that moment for her. I'm old enough now—but with that understanding comes guilt.

As an adult, I've gained a better perspective on the kind of person she was—though I'm sure I've barely scratched the surface of everything that she did for our family. One of the things that hurts most is that I didn't get to know her as an adult instead of exclusively as a mother. She never got to be anything *but* a mother for me. If I was crying back then, it was because of something bad. We never shared tears of joy from a piece of music or the ending to a film. And even worse, I didn't show enough appreciation for everything she did for me. Anytime I feel underappreciated in life, especially at my job as a high school teacher (which happens a lot, it's high school), I'm haunted by the number of times she must have felt the same. Again, the guilt of it all.

I don't have any videos of Mom. The closest I have is her voice on a VHS tape cheering for me during a 4th grade soccer game. But I don't need videos to remember her voice. Our family photo collection of her is disproportionately low, too. She was always the one taking the pictures. "Mom, look at me!"

It was never about her, until it was about being *without* her. I have to forgive myself for being a teenager. Every time I excuse a student for being ungrateful, it reminds me to take it easy on myself.

I wish Mom could have met my wife, Beth. They would've had fun exercising and cooking together. When my dad was a head basketball coach and someone in the stands bad-mouthed him, Mom didn't stay quiet. Beth is my biggest fan and is just as defensive on my behalf and honestly, the two of them together would've been amusingly dangerous together during one of my stand-up comedy shows. Anyone daring to heckle me would get a one-two combo much funnier than anything I could say. The odd thing is, I don't know if I ever would've become a comedian if Mom was still alive. I didn't need anyone else to hear me, as long as she did.

There are always hypothetical questions and answers, though I've stopped asking why. Here's the amazing thing, once I stopped asking—I actually found the answer. My Mom gave so much unconditional love to everyone she knew that her heart grew tired. A full lifetime of love got compressed down to the shorter amount of years God let her live on this Earth.

Going back to that Christmas Eve, I can't prove to anyone that those Christmas lights defied science and logic and shined so brightly in that mysterious way for that brief moment in time, but I can tell you that for fifteen years of my life, my mother did the same thing.

ACKNOWLEDGMENTS

Thank you to my wife, Beth, for her continued support in all of my careers. She has to hear about my books more than anyone else.

Thank you to Sioux Roslawski for all of the helpful feedback. You're a wonderful author and I invite everyone to read your novel, *Greenwood Gone: Henry's Story*. It's a fantastic and memorable read!

John Randle designed the book's cover. I didn't give him much to go on, and he turned it into a beautiful work of art.

Thank you to my other beta readers including Liz Pease, Austin Woods, Jennifer Shepherd, and all of my creative writing students at Marquette High School. It's not easy to get volunteer readers to follow through, so I appreciate your time and effort.

Finally, thank you to my father for reading very early drafts and encouraging me. My sister, Susan, and my brother, David, have always been supportive as well. I thank you and I love you.

ABOUT THE AUTHOR

Rob Durham is a high school golf coach, English teacher, stand-up comedian, and author of several books including *Don't Wear Shorts on Stage, Around the Block, Somebody Else's Sky,* and *Don't Do Shots with Strangers.* An Ohio native, he moved to St. Louis in 2005 and married his wife Beth a few years later.

When he's not in the classroom, Rob enjoys playing pickleball, attending Modest Mouse concerts, and taking Ohio State football games way too seriously. You can find his comedy tour schedule on RobDurhamComedy.com and follow him on social media @RobDurhamComedy.

Made in the USA
Monee, IL
21 April 2025

16089895R00118